SO THERE I WAS...

THE AFTER-ACTION SHORT STORIES OF A TEAM OF MANY: AXE, HALEY, NALEN, MAD DOG, AND OTHERS FROM THE UNSANCTIONED ASSET SERIES

BRAD LEE

INTRODUCTION

Author's Note

I wrote these short stories over the course of about eighteen months while writing *A Team of One, A Team of Two, A Team of Three, A Team of Four, A Team of Five,* and *A Team of Six.*

They were originally sent to some of my newsletter subscribers month by month, but I have decided to finally offer them in a book for people to read all at once.

Spoiler Alerts

Some of the following short stories contain material that gives away plot points of the preceding books. For the best experience, please read each book (in bold below and available via Amazon or by ordering through your favorite local bookstore) prior to the corresponding short story.

Reading Order/Chronology

- *A Team of One*
- *Operation Deadly Silence (Part 1)*

- *Operation Deadly Silence (Part 2)*
- ***A Team of Two***
- *Operation Dark Moon*
- ***A Team of Three***
- *Operation Swing Time*
- *Operation End Run*
- ***A Team of Four***
- *Operation Mad Dog*
- *Operation Past Due*
- *Operation Hammer Time*
- *Operation White Flag*
- ***A Team of Five***
- *Operation One Shot*
- *Operation White Stripe*
- *Operation First Kill*
- *Operation Battle Rattle*
- *Operation Sudden Fury*
- *Operation Cease Fire*
- ***A Team of Six***

Thanks for reading, and I hope you enjoy the short stories.

~ Brad

OPERATION DEADLY
SILENCE PART 1

1

ONE MORE

The gathering in this story takes place immediately after the ending of *A Team of One*. Please read it prior to starting this story.

Alex "Axe" Southmark's Cabin
Rural Virginia

Haley tipped her head back in the old leather chair by the fireplace. The embers were dying, but some warmth remained.

The active-member SEALs sat around Axe's old cabin in the woods, along with Admiral Nalen, Axe, and Mad Dog, after the recent operation in the Virgin Islands.

After a long night of laughter and camaraderie, the mood had quieted.

Between the stories, the beer, and a workout hitting the heavy punching bag earlier in the night, Haley couldn't keep her eyes open any longer.

And surrounded by these warriors, she felt safe for the first time in weeks.

The men laughed and spoke quietly, respectful of her sleepiness, but they were used to staying awake until dawn. She only pulled all-nighters when they were on operations requiring her support.

"Okay," Axe started, louder than they had been speaking, rousing her as she faded into sleep.

Haley sat up slowly, willing herself awake.

"This one's funny," he said with a smile. "So no shit, there we were—"

"No. Absolutely not." From the couch, Red shook his head.

"You don't even know what I'm going to say!"

"Operation Deadly Silence, right?"

The rest of the men were already chuckling.

"She needs to hear it," Ronbo said.

"Think of it as operational training," Thor agreed. "It might save her life someday."

Axe nodded but held back, waiting for Red's go-ahead.

"Operation Deadly Silence?" she asked Red. "How bad can it be?"

"It's not for mixed company," he said to resounding laughter.

"I know this woman," Axe pointed out. "The things she's seen and done? She can handle Deadly Silence."

"Promise not to think less of me," Red told her. The room was dim and his bushy red beard covered his face, but it certainly seemed like he was blushing.

"I promise."

"Me too," the others joined in solemnly, holding back their laughter.

Mad Dog chimed in. "I can't promise anything."

Red glared at him, and he quickly backpedaled. "Okay, I won't think less of you."

Admiral Nalen—"Hammer"—just sipped his beer and shook his head in amusement.

"Anyway, there we were—" Axe started again.

"If we're going to tell it," Red interrupted, setting his empty beer bottle on the coffee table, "tell it right."

"Fine. You start and I'll jump in if you try to skip the good parts. Don't forget the salsa."

Red took a deep breath, struggling for patience. "The salsa is beside the point. The problem," he told Haley, "was the beans."

"And the helicopter," Thor said.

"And the guard," Ronbo added.

"Gentlemen, what did I say?" Red asked them, frowning in mock seriousness.

Link's deep voice rumbled from the far side of the room. "I think it's called foreshadowing. But let him tell it his way."

Hiding their laughter, the men agreed and sat quietly as Red started again. "First, Haley, let's get this out of the way. I didn't fall all the way out of the helicopter."

2

DEADLY SILENCE

Alex "Axe" Southmark's Cabin
Rural Virginia

Haley was tired but welcomed the story from these warriors.

Last one for tonight, then I'm off to bed, she thought.

"We'll start at the beginning," Red said, accepting a cold beer from Thor. "It was Cinco de Mayo and—"

"Wait, Hector, when is that again? Late April, right?" Ronbo joked.

"You nailed it, Ronbo. Late April or early May, depending on the lunar cycle," Hector said with a shake of his head.

"It was Thor's first year with us," Red continued, ignoring the banter. "He made a sample plate of authentic food to go with the mess hall dinner."

"I got up early and used my grandmother's recipes," Thor told Haley. "I'll bring a few dishes next time."

Red put his head in his hands. The guys hooted and hollered.

Thor winked at her. "And milk. Someone remind me."

"The real problem is the mess hall ran out of milk," Red explained.

Link added, "We slept all day while the base around us functioned normally. Most people were up and awake, doing their jobs. They must have drunk all the milk."

"Turns out my grandmother's recipes were a bit too spicy for the delicate flower over here," Thor said, nodding to Red.

"Delicate flower—that's a good one," Red grumbled.

"Should be your new call sign," Thor said. "'Go for Flower Actual,'" he said, imitating Red's drawl.

Red gave him a cold, drop-dead look. Thor shut up immediately.

"Where was I, Haley?"

"Milk."

"Right, so the food tasted amazing. We all devoured it."

"Scraped the plates," Thor said with pride.

"I'm no delicate flower, and I didn't have a problem with it."

"At first!" the gang chimed in, aside from Admiral Nalen, who hadn't been there—he'd been the overall commanding officer but wasn't with the front-line Teams.

"At first," Red agreed. "So we do our mission brief, gear up, and load into the chopper. Eight of us for a medium-length flight and a long hike in."

"The target was a suspected money man for a terrorist group," Ronbo explained. "We didn't expect many enemy tangos, but this guy was more sophisticated than the usual farmer or goat herder turned freedom fighter: a solid house with alert guards, the whole deal."

"And the name of the op was really 'Deadly Silence'?" Haley had to ask.

"No," Ron continued. "It's the name we gave it afterwards. Anyone remember the real name?"

No one did.

"We're in the chopper, and I get a pang," Red said, his voice quieting. "Something's not right in the gut—you know that feeling?" He looked queasy just remembering.

She nodded. "All too well." She'd made the mistake of having fish at a home-style chain restaurant while on a road trip a few years before. It had seemed fine at the time—but when the first pang hit, she knew it had been a terrible choice.

"But we're in a helicopter on our way to capture a bad guy. What am I going to do?"

"What are you gonna do?" the guys said, shaking their heads while chuckling.

"And SEALs are tough," Link said in his slow, quiet voice. "We can take whatever you dish out."

"Not what *Abuela* dishes out, though!" Ron said, using the Spanish word for "grandmother."

"I swear I actually put less spice in than the recipe calls for," Thor whispered to her.

"Picture this," Red continued. "We're in the bird. I'm at the back. Cold night, we're going quite a way, so we've got the door closed."

"Not for long," Thor muttered.

"Right. First thing: sorry, Haley. This is locker-room talk. It's why I didn't want to tell the story."

Haley nodded and guessed what was coming. With her face serious, she told him, "Thanks for the warning. Girls never pass gas. It's our code."

The guys cracked up.

Not hilarious, but it's the mood in the room. A stand-up comedian would have them crying tears of laughter tonight.

"At first, we joked about it—making faces, fanning the air, having fun," Ron said.

"SEALs are tough," Link repeated.

"But after a while…" Ron said with a grimace.

"I think we all would have rung the bell to make it stop," Axe chimed in. "And remember, we don't quit."

I remember.

Axe had suffered a punctured lung, a bullet in his head, and had lost damn near all the blood in his body. But he still dived into the ocean and held onto a submarine in a futile attempt to catch the bad guy.

"I'm aware," she said dryly. Several of the Team looked at Axe and nodded their respect for him.

"Simple solution," Red continued. "We open the door."

"Cold, but at least we can breathe," Link said.

Red hesitated, not wanting to continue.

"You tell it or we will," Axe warned.

"Fine." Red's shoulders slumped.

He's not faking this for the story. He's still embarrassed.

"This is where he falls out of the chopper," Thor whispered to her.

THE HELICOPTER

Alex "Axe" Southmark's Cabin
Rural Virginia

"I did not fall out of the helicopter!" Red roared, which made the men laugh hysterically. Haley tried to hold her laughter back but couldn't. Red's exasperation was just too funny.

"True," Axe explained. "He didn't fall all the way out of the helicopter."

"We had to shuffle around to get him near the door," Link said slowly. He mimed moving his gear, holding his rifle carefully out of the way.

"And we had to do it much quicker than that!" Thor added.

Ronbo said seriously, "We thought about asking the chopper pilot to land, but…"

"'Don't make me pull this helicopter over,'" Axe said in his best imitation of an exasperated father.

"We normally only use the safety tethers if the helicopter is dodging fire," Red explained. "But it seemed like a good idea, given what I planned. So I wrapped one around my waist and clipped another into my chest harness."

"Two is one and one is none," the group chanted in unison, even Mad Dog and Hammer.

"Then I backed up, pulled my pants down, squatted, and hung my rear over the edge."

"If it were only so easy," Thor whispered to her.

Haley was enraptured. *A natural process? Yes. Gross? Definitely. But a hell of a story!*

Red looked more embarrassed, staring down and hiding his face behind his beer bottle. "Hey, did we ever tell you about the time the drug lord's wife came on to Axe? We were in—"

"No," Axe interrupted. "We've heard about me. This one is all you, my friend."

They waited in anticipation while he mustered the courage to continue.

How do I ask this delicately? Haley wondered.

"It didn't... you know... back into the helicopter, did it?"

She was greeted with groans of disgust and exaggerated exclamations of horror from the group.

"Haley, that's disgusting!" Thor said. Turning to Axe, he asked, "Where did you get her? She's pretty, yes, but come on!"

It was her turn to blush. "Sorry! Okay—what happened then?"

"I couldn't go," Red admitted. "But in my defense, we were flying through the dark, my ass is hanging out the door of the bird, and I've got seven other guys—"

"Plus the pilots," Axe added. "They were totally checking out the situation."

"Yes, plus the pilots—all watching me. That cleared it up faster than any Loperamide could."

She looked at Ronbo for clarification. "Antidiarrheal medicine," he said.

"Tell her the next part," Axe encouraged.

"Fine. The pilots claim it was turbulence, and I can't believe they did it on purpose, but..."

Axe nodded. "Had to be turbulence."

"The bird tilted just enough that I lost my balance," Red admitted, staring into space.

"It happened so suddenly none of us could grab him," Thor said.

"I instinctively straightened my legs to tighten the safety straps. I guess I didn't want to fall and dangle below the helicopter."

"We would have had to pull him back in. Land the chopper, even," Ron said.

"But I knew the tethers would hold me if I could pull against them before I fell."

"So he stands up suddenly, like he's deadlifting a lighter weight than expected. Just shoots upwards," Axe said, giggling like a little kid.

Suddenly, she could picture it. "No," she said, covering her mouth with shock and trying to hide her laughter.

"You've seen how much gear we carry in our pockets," Link said.

"Makes the pants heavy," Mad Dog nodded, chuckling. "Oh man, I can just see it."

Hammer shook his head with a grin from across the room. "Son, tell me you didn't drop your pants in the door of the helicopter."

Red raised his head, looking at the ceiling. "With God as my witness, there I stood, pants and briefs around my ankles, leaning back at a forty-five-degree angle, on my tippy toes, holding the tight straps in a death grip."

The men were crying with laughter, except for Link, who said with all seriousness, "It was the funniest thing I've seen in my life."

"He looked like he was in a high-tech, X-rated rodeo!" Thor choked out between laughs.

"Ride 'em, cowboy!" Ronbo called.

The room dissolved into uncontrollable laughter, and Haley joined them.

4

DAWN

Haley waited for the story to continue as Red shook his head at the memory.

When the laughter finally quieted, Red looked up. "I pulled myself in. Yanked up my pants. Closed the damn door. My intestinal issues were gone."

"For a while," Link once again muttered to her with a wink.

"I've been shot at—and shot. I've jumped out of airplanes and climbed mountain faces. I even caught a grenade a tango asshole threw at us—and tossed it back to him."

"That was scary," Link admitted.

"But I have never been as terrified as when I leaned out of the helicopter that night. Not so much for fear of dying—though, let me tell you, it felt like I was going to plummet to the ground—but the embarrassment. Fear of my backside choosing to let go right then. Losing my pants, though realistically there's no way they could have slipped over my boots. Or just falling out, dangling from the bird and causing such a scene I'd hear about it for the rest of my days..."

"Well, hearing about it for years has actually come to pass," Thor said with a big grin.

"Just like the beans," Ronbo added.

Haley dried her eyes. Her stomach ached from laughing so hard.

What's the protocol here? Do I tell him I'm sorry it happened to him? Offer him a hug? Around the room, the men were smiling at Red. Respect and admiration shone in their eyes. *Good. We're letting off steam and laughing with him, not at him.*

"To this day, I don't know whether it was the spiciness of the salsa, the cumin in the black beans, or the cilantro that did it. I can eat other Mexican food, no problem, just not whatever *Abuela* puts in hers."

They all took a moment to sip beers and relax after the laughter.

I've never felt closer to another group of people, Haley realized.

Eventually, Axe spoke up. "Tell her about the gifts."

"And the improvements," Thor suggested.

Red nodded matter-of-factly. "Right. The next day we upgraded the helicopter."

Link said, "I insisted. I don't ever again want to see him with his ass hanging out, looking at me while trying to go."

"Or the naked helicopter-bucking-bronco routine," Thor chimed in.

"Let alone thinking we could have lost him if he fell out of the chopper," Axe said seriously, almost too quiet to hear.

They took a second to acknowledge the sentiment, then all joined in with Red as he said, "Not all the way out of the helicopter!"

They laughed again as Red continued. "They scrounged up a five-gallon bucket and camouflage paint. Our chopper suddenly had a toilet."

"Plus sturdy plastic bags, a roll of toilet paper, and wet wipes."

"So if you ever see a military helicopter with a bucket, it's because of Red," Axe said with pride.

"And the gifts?" Haley asked.

"Still coming from time to time. First was a cowboy hat. Then every brand of Loperamide out there."

"Extra, extra strength," Thor said. "Military-grade."

"And adult diapers," Ronbo added.

"Which came in handy, you have to admit," Red said, looking pointedly at many of the men.

"True. We've been on a few very long missions," Thor muttered.

"Things like that. But I've gotten them gifts, too: gas masks, clothespins." He pinched his nose.

"Jarred salsa," Thor said with disgust. "Mild heat!" He rolled his eyes.

The rising sun shone through the window, lighting up Red's face. He shielded his eyes with his hand and paused.

She had to know how it ended. "How was the op? Once the helicopter landed, were you able to... you know. Go? In the bushes or wherever?"

Red couldn't hold back a yawn. He stretched. "That's for another time." He checked with the rest of the guys, who all looked tired now, too.

"Yep, time for bed," Ron said. "You won't believe it, anyway."

"Yes, unbelievable," Thor added. "We had an experimental weapon along. We never thought it would work, but..."

"The military should've fast-tracked the development of it," Link muttered. "What a waste."

They were shining her on. She could tell. Men had done it all her life, telling her lies and half-truths, trying to get dates with her.

They're acting so serious, though. Could I be wrong?

"Call it 'Operation Deadly Silence, Part Two.' We'll tell you sometime," Ronbo promised.

"Time for bed," Axe said, standing. "I'll show you your room," he told Haley.

5

WARRIORS

Alex "Axe" Southmark's Cabin
Rural Virginia

She said good night to the guys, watching with surprise as they all pitched in to clean up the mess of beer bottles and dinner plates. Then she followed Axe down a short hallway at the back of the cabin.

He stopped outside a closed door. "I have an apology to make."

Uh-oh.

"Two, actually."

"Okay..."

"Red wanted to ask you out—he made it clear when we on the Mexico op. I hated the idea, which is my first apology. It's not my place to discourage—or encourage—anybody around dating you. I'm sorry. It won't happen again."

Red and me? No. Never. Not my type. But it's true, he should stay out of my love life. She played it cool. "Apology accepted. What else?"

"If you were interested in him..." He held his hands up. "I don't want to know. But I blew it for the two of you. By inviting him here tonight or, rather, bringing you into the group, I ruined it. I don't have to ask to know how he feels about you now. How they all feel about you."

What did I do? Not that I'm interested in any of them, but still.

"Did I put him—or the others—off?"

"No, not at all. On the contrary. They love you. But all of us think of you as one of the guys now. Well," he corrected, "that might be a stretch. But they look at you as I do. You're a sister warrior. I'm sorry. If you were interested in any of them, I've messed it up."

It felt amazing to be considered a part of this group. Contrary to ruining everything, Axe had made her day, her week. Her year.

I'm not going to cry, she thought, forcing herself to hold back tears of gratitude. "Thanks, Axe. I'm good," she said, putting on her game face. "None of the guys interest me that way. And I'm happy to be the warrior sister."

Axe relaxed, then offered her a fist bump. She brushed it aside and gave him a strong—brotherly—bear hug. "You're a great partner, Axe."

He briefly hugged her back. "You too," he said gruffly. Then he showed her the small spare bedroom, nodded, and shut the door quietly as he left.

By the time she got ready and climbed into the perfectly made bed, a cacophony of snores came from the living room where her new brothers slept.

———————

———————

OPERATION DEADLY
SILENCE PART 2

1

BREAKFAST

Alex "Axe" Southmark's Cabin
Rural Virginia

Axe watched with pleasure as his former SEAL teammates devoured the eggs, bacon, toast, and pancakes he'd made for breakfast, along with coffee. They spoke quietly, respectful of Haley, who was still sound asleep in the spare bedroom. Axe sat down at the far end of the table to join them.

"Feels good to be here. Thanks for hosting, Axe," Red said. "Wish you were still in the field with us."

It wasn't the first time Red had expressed the sentiment.

"Best of both worlds," Axe said, topping up Red's mug. "I tag along on a mission here and there while you guys go save the world full time."

"Here, here," the active-duty Team murmured.

"Morning," Haley said, coming into the dining area, rubbing the sleep from her eyes, her hair in a sloppy ponytail.

"Morning," each of them said. Haley's gray sweatpants and baggy gray sweatshirt hid her figure, but nothing could disguise her beauty, even with bed head and no makeup.

Most of these guys would love someone like her—but not her, Axe thought. *Not anymore.*

After last night, telling stories, laughing, and bonding together, she was one of them. Off-limits, though Red had already asked Axe if she had a sister.

"Coffee," Axe said, getting a large mug from the cupboard and filling it for her. She took it gratefully as Thor and Ronbo scooted closer together on the bench seat of Axe's long table, giving her room to join them.

Axe got her a plate. She dug in while the men chatted around her.

Come on, Axe silently begged her. *Wait a few more minutes.*

He checked the clock on the microwave, hoping she could hold out longer.

I think she can sense it.

Haley had amazing intuition. But did it work in the real world, or was it limited to sitting in front of a computer, swimming through data?

She finished a pancake, then asked the question they had all been waiting for. "So—Operation Deadly Silence, Part Two?"

Damn it. Missed it by one minute!

The group of men sat still, not knowing exactly how to handle the next part.

"You think I can't tell you've got something going? A bet, right? Go ahead and settle up," Haley said, grabbing more bacon and glaring at them in mock anger.

"How the hell does she do it, Axe?" Red asked him, pulling a ten-dollar bill out of his wallet and slapping it on the table.

"No idea," he said, adding his own bill.

The rest of the men did the same: Mad Dog, Thor, Ronbo, and Link. All except Admiral Nalen—Hammer—who sat quietly at the end of the table with a small smile, sipping his coffee. The admiral stretched forward, gathered up the money, and gave thirty dollars to Haley.

"What's going on, gentlemen?" Haley asked, accepting the money from Nalen.

"We had an over-under bet on how long it would take you to ask for the rest of the story," Axe explained. "Sorry."

"You all lost? The admiral won?" She looked at Nalen. "You chose under?"

Nalen nodded, folding the money carefully and putting it in the pocket of his blue jeans. He had on yet another perfectly white, unwrinkled T-shirt.

Where the hell does he get them? He must have an ironed stack in his truck.

"Yes, I had under," Nalen said. "I took the sure thing."

Haley considered his answer. Axe did too.

"How was the under a sure thing, Hammer?" Axe asked.

"And why didn't you let me in on that?" Mad Dog said to plenty of laughter.

"He knew I'd sense the bet," Haley said, looking respectfully at Nalen. "Smart. You all have to remember I've spent my life having guys lie and say anything to get with me. I know when men are shining me on."

"No man will ever do it again—not if we're with you," Link rumbled from the other end of the table.

She looked at Axe.

He nodded at her. "Not on my watch."

"Thanks, guys," she said, and took more food than Axe thought she could ever eat and started to work her way through it. "So," she said, her mouth half full, "you going to tell me or not?"

Red's head dropped, and he sighed. "It doesn't get any better."

"What could be better than you mooning the world, waiting for your bowels to let go?" Thor asked as they all regained the humor from the night before. "Before falling out of the helicopter."

He said it to get a rise out of him, which Red well knew, but it worked as intended.

They all joined in as Red bellowed, "I did not fall all the way out of the helicopter!"

It took several seconds for the room to calm down from the

hysterical laughter, time that Axe used to top up coffee cups and slide onto the bench seat across the table from Haley.

"So no shit, there we were," Axe began as the group quieted, which produced another fit of laughter.

"Well, a lot of shit, actually," Thor said to Haley under his breath.

"We were finally on the ground, watching our sectors, wondering if Red had to find a convenient bush or if his naked cowboy helicopter rodeo stunt had clamped him down," Axe said and remembered.

2

THE APPROACH

Many Years Earlier
Somewhere in the Middle East

Axe knelt, gun up, focused on the area in front of him. The dark night felt safe. It hid them, and with their NVGs, they had an edge over the enemy. But next came a long walk, first through dangerous territory, then into a city, which presented its own challenges.

And there was the problem with their leader's bowels.

"You okay? You going to be able to keep it together?" Axe whispered to Red, kneeling next to him. Although Red was the team lead, Axe had been a SEAL several years longer. They had a good dynamic. Red gave the orders, but occasionally he turned to Axe for quiet, unofficial guidance. And Axe looked after the younger leader.

"Fine," Red said curtly. Then he softened. "But... I'll bring up the rear this time."

Normally, Red would be the third or fourth man back, close enough to the front—and action—to see unfolding events, but far enough back to lead the Team without having to immediately engage the enemy.

"It's still bothering you?" Axe asked. A second later, he realized he didn't need to ask. The smell hit him. "Geez, Red. Seriously, that's not good."

"I know, I know. But it is what it is."

"It is what it is."

"Let's go," Red said into his mic, which broadcast to the entire Team. "Axe, take point."

Axe was already oriented on their planned path, so he made sure the men were ready and started forward.

They were on the outskirts of a small city in the desert, far enough away no one had cared about their bird dropping them off. American forces were all over the region. The sound of a helicopter in the middle of the night wasn't uncommon.

Until now, though, there had been little patrolling through their target neighborhood. An upper-middle-class enclave, it had escaped much of the violence of the rest of the city and country. For whatever reason, the bad guys avoided the area. Because there was no enemy to engage, the American forces didn't waste time there.

In the Team's cynical theory, though, all the enemy leaders secretly lived in the area. They kept the lower level riffraff far away—and the area free of violence—so they'd be safe from American scrutiny and patrols.

Tonight, the Team would turn on a light and see how many roaches ran away.

Their target lived in a nice, modern home with solid walls and doors, according to the intel.

No mud huts here.

Other houses—full of civilians—surrounded the target, which made tonight's operation especially difficult. The Team had to breach a door, kill or silence the guard who reportedly sat just inside, and get to the second floor, where the man they were to capture had his bedroom and office… along with other guards, they guessed.

And they had to do it quietly, without disturbing the affluent neighbors—and especially without killing any of them.

And without letting the guards shoot, which could easily miss the Team and hit an innocent bystander.

Alex "Axe" Southmark's Cabin
Rural Virginia

"The only easy day was yesterday," Axe said. The others around the breakfast table repeated the mantra. Haley mouthed the words, though she didn't speak aloud.

I have to tell her it's okay for her to join in on that one, Axe thought. *She's definitely earned it—and lived it.*

"So what happened during the long walk in, Red? Were you okay?" Haley asked. She sounded so caring. It was almost hard to believe the number of enemy she'd killed.

Red shook his head. "It was touch and go. Whatever held me together in the helicopter—"

"Like the pilots watching you?" Thor interrupted.

"Whatever," Red said. "It deserted me during the hike to the X. But I knew I couldn't go to the bathroom."

"No…" Ronbo said.

"Tell it right, or we will," Axe had to remind him.

"Fine." He sighed theatrically. "Haley, these guys—this is more than you should hear, as a lady—"

Mad Dog snorted under his breath, and they all glared at him until he apologized. "Sorry, Haley."

"But the truth is, I knew once I started going, I'd have to stay very close to a bathroom."

We all know the feeling, Axe thought.

"Been there, done that," Haley said, to much surprised laughter.

She truly is one of the guys.

"So I stayed at the back during the hike in."

"And probably woke up half the neighborhood leaving behind a trail of stench," Thor whispered with a huge smile.

"Which is what gave me the idea," Axe said.

3

THE DOOR

Alex "Axe" Southmark's Cabin
Rural Virginia

"For once, the intel was right," Axe continued. "The house was well built, the door sturdy. Metal. Solid lock and deadbolt."

"We would have had to blow the whole thing off its hinges to get in," Link said.

"Link was our breacher," Axe explained to Haley. "He would have nailed it, no problem."

"But the noise…" Haley said.

"Exactly. It would have woken up the entire neighborhood," Ronbo said.

Many Years Earlier
Somewhere in the Middle East

Axe stacked up behind Link at the door. In the night vision goggles, he watched Link assess the situation, then step to the other side of the doorway and silently unsling his pack for the explosives he'd need.

Explosives... Axe thought.

Axe got Link's attention and, using hand signals, communicated he should continue preparing, but they were going to try something else first.

Behind him, Ronbo and Thor waited, their guns trained outward. Up and down the street, and on the block behind the house, watching the rear, the rest of the Team stood guard.

Axe gestured for Red to come up, not using his mic to whisper in case the intel was right for once and a guard sat just inside the door.

Red showed no surprise at being summoned. As the team lead, he dealt with any unusual situations the four-man entry team couldn't resolve themselves.

Using only hand signals, Axe explained what he wanted to try.

Red scowled, but Axe wasn't joking. They stared at each other—or at each other's NVGs. A battle of wills. Red broke first. He moved ahead of Axe to stand with his rear end nearly touching the door.

Link stepped back.

Axe stepped back.

A few seconds later, Axe smelled it. His eyes watered instantly. *It's worse now than in the chopper*, he thought.

On the other side of the doorway, Link looked like he was about to heave.

It was like something had died inside of Red.

He moved closer to the hinges and let go two more times, forcing Link and Axe to move back farther.

From inside, a scuffling noise. Red silently stepped out of the way as Link and Axe moved back into position.

The deadbolt unlocked.

The lock on the knob clicked, then it turned.

Link kept his M4 ready while Axe prepared to strike.

A young guard's face appeared as he cracked open the door. He looked horrified as he stuck his head out to investigate the stench.

Axe slammed the butt of his rifle into him, knocking him out cold. Link caught the guard as he fell.

Red stepped forward to grab the limp body so Link and Axe could enter.

Ronbo helped Red drag the man away for one of the other guys to flex cuff, gag, and secure down the street, away from the action.

And like that, they were inside.

4

THE HOUSE

Axe finished telling the first part of the story and paused to drink his coffee. Remembering the old days made him long for them.

Getting out when I did was the right move, I know, but I miss it.

At least the men were still his brothers.

Haley stared at them, spellbound but disbelieving. "You're kidding," she told the assembled warriors at the table. "Right?"

"What does your gut tell you?" Thor asked, serious for a change.

Haley stared at each of their faces. "My hunch is you're telling the truth."

Axe nodded, as did Ronbo, Red, Thor, and Link.

"God's honest truth," Link said. "The smell nearly killed me. I don't know how much made it under the door or through the hinges or wherever, but it made the guard curious enough to open it."

"Incredible," Haley said. "And that's it? You got the guy and got out?"

"If it were only that easy..." Axe said.

"But don't worry, we all make it out okay," Thor assured her with mock seriousness.

Haley rolled her eyes.

"Thankfully, we had our experimental weapon along," Thor said. "Or it could have ended much differently."

Axe took one last sip of his cooling coffee and resumed the story. "Intel had said there were only four guards," he said.

"The intel is always wrong," the men said together, except for Nalen.

Haley frowned.

"Except when Haley's in charge," Hammer said from the end of the table.

The men raised their coffee mugs and toasted Haley, which she accepted with a small smile.

"Actually, they were right this time," Axe continued.

"And wrong," Ronbo said.

"Yes, and wrong. They didn't know about the other doors."

Many Years Earlier
Somewhere in the Middle East

Axe silently stepped through the doorway, leading with his suppressed short-barrel M4. The weak overhead light in the small space overwhelmed his NVGs, so he popped them up onto his helmet and waited a second for his eyes to adjust.

Ahead lay a long hallway. At the end, another door.

What do you do when you don't want a bunch of armed guards hanging around a nice neighborhood? Instead of leaving them out in the open, I bet you put each one behind a locked door.

Having to breech several doors would give their target time to destroy his computers—the ones the intel nerds desperately wanted. It would also give him time to escape. The Team had the back of the house and the roof covered, but there could be a tunnel or a hidden room.

Or a quick reaction force on call in a nearby house.

Before going farther down the hall, Axe gestured to Link, who passed along the signal to Ronbo, then to Thor standing right outside.

Seconds later, Red entered, his body language showing it all: physical discomfort, embarrassment, and reluctance.

Axe nodded at the next door, his intention clear, and led the way down the hall.

Red refined the technique at the second barrier. He squatted, careful to do so silently, until his rear end sat near the small gap under the door.

Axe stood within inches of him, prepared to shoot or club the guard he suspected was on the other side.

This time, there was no escaping the smell. Axe's eyes watered, and he repeatedly fought against gagging for thirty agonizing seconds. Then there was movement from behind the door.

Red stood and squeezed in behind Axe, pushing Link back to third man.

They were ready.

Once again, the door opened quietly and another guard poked his head and shoulders out, a disgusted look on his face.

Axe slammed the butt of his rifle into the man's head. Red caught the guard before he could fall and make noise.

They were through the second door.

Got another one.

On the other side were stairs. At the top of the stairs, another door.

The next two doors worked the same. Red gassed the guard, and Axe knocked him out when he opened the door to see what had caused the horrible smell.

Suckers.

Alex "Axe" Southmark's Cabin
Rural Virginia

"The target was asleep in his bedroom," Axe told Haley. "We slipped in, gagged and bagged him, and—"

"Bagged him?" Haley asked.

"Put a thick black bag over his head," Ronbo explained.

"We had plenty of time to pull his hard drives, gather his notebooks, and even found his safe," Axe said.

"Between the target, the guards, and the haul from the office, we changed the plan," Red said. "I called in a second chopper. They both landed at a small city park a few blocks away."

"Much better than a long walk out, dragging the bad guys," Thor added.

"But the most brilliant idea of all was Axe's," Link said, his deep voice full of respect.

Axe shrugged humbly.

Haley looked from one to the other and asked, "What idea?"

"We made Red ride in the chopper with the prisoners!" Thor said to cheering from the rest of the guys.

"I took the bag off the target's head once we had him secured in the helicopter," Red admitted, "and sat right next to him. The pilots did something to keep the smell from affecting them—opened a vent or whatever. By the time we returned to base, the target looked green—and it wasn't from my NVGs."

"He begged to talk to the intel guys—anything to not be stuck with Red any longer," Axe said.

"We thought about sending a report of our secret weapon to our former instructors at BUD/S," Thor said, "to use it during training as a way to separate the men from the boys."

"Too many guys would quit, though. We'd be responsible for losing a whole class of future warriors, so we didn't dare," Link said.

"I mentioned it to the intel guys, a few days later, when I felt better," Red said. "They were intrigued."

"It's not a bad idea," Haley agreed. "Using smells to pique interest or distract."

"If you have time, and the bad guys are curious or concerned, it works well," Ronbo said. "With the right scent."

"We could be rich," Thor said with a big grin. "You and me, Red. I feed you *Abuela*'s dishes, they monitor you and find out how to reproduce the smells!"

"The food's delicious, my friend, but I'm never eating your grandmother's recipes again," Red said. "No offense."

"None taken. But next time, we get plenty of milk. And I'll set some of the food aside for you before I add the spice. The 'delicate flower' version."

Red held up a lone finger—but he smiled.

"Speaking of delicate flowers," Axe said, looking at Haley. "Not too much for you?"

"I'm a delicate flower?" she asked with a laugh. Shaking her head, she answered. "It was definitely too much," she said. "But I loved it." She looked at Red with a heartfelt smile. "Sorry it happened, but you turned it around. Made the best of it."

"Adapt and overcome," Red said with a nod.

"And it makes a great story," Axe added. He raised his mug. "To Operation Deadly Silence." Everyone joined him. "And *Abuela*," he said, with a nod at Thor.

They clinked mugs, drained them, and set about cleaning up the kitchen Axe had destroyed making breakfast.

———————

———————

OPERATION DARK MOON

STRAIGHT TO HELL

The gathering in this story takes place immediately after the ending of *A Team of Two*. To avoid spoilers, please read it prior to this story.

Alex "Axe" Southmark's Cabin

Rural Virginia

The group had long since finished their afternoon "breakfast," cleaned up, and lingered over coffee. The time at Axe's cabin had been both fun and healing, especially for Haley.

I feel like I can get back to work and handle life again, thanks to these guys, Haley thought.

Finally, it was time to go. The men would return to their wives, girlfriends, families, or buddies. On Monday, the active-duty SEALs would be right back at training before their next deployment. Mad Dog would do whatever he did when he didn't have a private security client, which Haley suspected was hanging out, drinking beer, and not taking the world very seriously.

Admiral Nalen would... what? For all the time they'd worked

together, Haley didn't have much of a grasp on who he was or what he did in his free time.

Haley would go back to her quiet home outside DC and prepare for another week at the CAG, searching for threats, protecting the world.

No one wanted the time together to end, but Mad Dog and Nalen were the first to go. After they left, the rest of the Team gathered their gear and left as a group.

But once they were all out on the porch, Red spoke up. "One last story. A quick one. So—"

"Oh, no, you don't," Axe interrupted.

Red and the others were already laughing. "Payback is a bitch, my friend," Red said.

"It's only fair," Link said with a note of finality. And like that, it was settled, though no one sat down or went inside for more coffee. Instead, they leaned against the exterior of the cabin or the thick logs holding up the front porch, watching Red and Axe standing near the stairs.

Axe shook his head in resigned annoyance, struggling to hide a smile.

"How do you always know which story the other is going to tell?" Haley asked.

Red shrugged, but Axe spoke up. "As soon as I told you about Operation Deadly Silence, I knew he'd bring this one up before I got rid of him today," he said. "All I ask—"

"Is that we remember—he was young," the others said together.

"But hardly innocent," Red muttered with a grin. "But this goes no further," he said seriously. "This is guy talk. Wives or girlfriends don't find out. Deal?"

"He means you can't tell Connie," Axe told Haley, clarifying.

"She doesn't know?" Haley asked.

"Well, she knows the basics, but not the details."

Is he blushing? she wondered. "Deal. I'll keep it to myself," she told them.

"Great." Red said, then began the account as they did all their best stories. "So no shit, there we were…"

Haley waited for them to say where the operation took place, but once again, they wouldn't. *My security clearance is higher than any of theirs. Don't they realize I could look up the after-action report of their missions whenever I want?* But she was beginning to understand her role—she was the audience. Every story needs someone to hear it, and these men had told the same stories to one another for years. Having her around made it better for them—and a ton of fun for her.

And I'm learning a lot. This is a master class in combat, camaraderie, along with many things to do—and not do—on a mission.

With a quiet sigh, she gave in. "Where were you this time? The desert again?" she guessed.

"If we told you—" Thor said with a laugh, but she interrupted him.

"I know, you'd have to kill me?"

This made all the men crack up. "No… But we wouldn't get to see the annoyed expression on your face when we won't tell you where it happened!" Thor added.

She shook her head.

I walked right into that one.

"Let's just say it was opposite of the desert. Humid."

"So the jungle," she muttered, expecting another round of laughter at her eager interest, but they fell quiet.

"As usual, it started out fine…" Red said.

"And went straight to hell from there," Axe finished.

"Damn helicopters," Ronbo said from near the front door.

"It's not so much the choppers," Link added in his deep voice. "It's just they're always shot at."

"Big, slow, appealing targets for the bad guys," Ronbo agreed.

"We were eight guys in two choppers because we hoped to bring people out with us," Red said as the others started chuckling again and looking at Axe, who waved at them dismissively.

"If you keep laughing, you're going to give away the ending," he said with a fake scowl.

"If she's as smart as we think she is, she already knows what's coming," Red said, looking at her expectantly.

She considered the obvious challenge.

He's blushing, they're giving him a hard time, and I can't tell Connie, his girlfriend. It doesn't take a genius analyst to figure it out.

"It's about a woman," she said.

"Man, what a woman," Thor whispered, and the entire Team stopped for a second and stared into the distance, remembering.

2

THE MOUNTAIN

Alex "Axe" Southmark's Cabin

Rural Virginia

Haley settled in for the story, curious about what could possibly make Alex "Axe" Southmark blush.

"The intel had said the up-and-coming drug lord had a military background," Axe explained. "He recruited good men, trained them, and treated them well. In return, they were professional and loyal to him. But every full moon, the intel nerds claimed, he let half of them have a party, knowing no enemy in their right mind would attempt to assault his jungle hideaway on the brightest night of the month."

"With the thick jungle, the high mountains surrounding his valley, and only one—well-guarded—road into the area, it would be suicide to choose that night for an attack," Red agreed.

"He didn't understand the level of commitment the Navy SEALs have—or that we love a challenge," Link said.

"The five of us and three others were finishing up a training rotation and were scheduled to return to the Sandbox shortly," Axe said. "But we were tasked with an urgent mission: to capture a high-value target in the jungle of Colombia: Sebastian. A very bad guy.

Drugs, mostly, but what brought us to him was the money laundering. He was a financial genius."

"He'd gained the trust of the other major drug barons and cleaned their money," Ronbo explained.

Haley got it. "Capture him, and you get access to all the accounts," she said, admiring the plan. "What was the operation's name?" she asked, knowing it would make looking up the report easier if she ever wanted to check how far they strayed from the truth as they told her these tall tales.

"Operation Dark Moon," Red said, shaking his head. "Which was irony, I suppose, given it was the brightest damn moon in months."

"We flew into the valley through a high mountain pass," Axe said. The other guys seemed fine with letting him tell the story, but she suspected it would change once he got to the good parts.

Axe rode in the second chopper. They hadn't exactly drawn straws, but each of them had been aware of the risk. On one hand, the first bird through the pass might attract the most attention from alert sentries. On the other, the second bird through might be a better target for RPGs or other, more destructive weapons, which took a few extra seconds to prepare.

"We stood as a group," Red said, "glanced at each other, and each made our way to the helicopter we felt would be the best bet. I was last, ending up with Axe in the rear chopper less by choice and more because, as the leader, I had to balance out the numbers. Four men had already chosen to go in the first bird, so I got in the second one."

But given the height of the mountains, he explained, the noise of the helicopters, and the bright moon, both choppers were shot at. As several of the men in the first one had guessed, though, the second caught the brunt of the fire.

Axe and Red exchanged glances before turning toward the front yard and the woods beyond it as they remembered that night.

Many Years Earlier
The Jungle, Colombia

"Looks like we're going in hard," Red yelled over the wail of the engine as the pilots struggled to avoid crashing into the side of the mountain.

"No way, we're gonna make it!" Axe said. He'd had a good feeling about the night from the start, and a little enemy gunfire and the smell of smoke from the engine wasn't going to ruin his night.

"You're crazy. You know that, right?" Red said to him as the skid underneath them clipped the top of a tree.

All Axe could do was shrug. "I feel lucky tonight," he said.

They went weightless a moment later as they cleared the pass—leaving behind the gunfire—and the pilot dropped abruptly toward the valley floor. The night was too bright, they had lost the element of surprise when sentries stationed in the pass had heard and seen them, and they were aiming straight for the well-guarded jungle home of a notorious drug lord.

"At least half of the guards will be drunk!" Axe yelled to Red.

3

THE ASSAULT

Alex "Axe" Southmark's Cabin
Rural Virginia

"If they hadn't been drunk out of their minds, we never would have made it out alive," Link rumbled from where he stood on the front steps. Although he was below the level of the porch, Haley still had to look up at him. His immense bulk and rough features, partly hidden by a big, bushy beard and hair in need of a trim, disguised a gentle, caring man... who would kill in an instant to fulfill his mission.

"Our door gunner," Red said, "Garrity, trained the big Gatling gun on the compound and mowed down people while Ron and the guys fast-roped in. Then their bird covered us. Honestly, the Gatlings did much of the heavy lifting."

"Love those things," Link muttered.

"We assaulted the building, this ornate mansion in the jungle, completely out of place," Red continued. "Link took out the door."

"Needed a big charge on it. Solid. But I blew the sucker off its hinges," Link said proudly.

"Which took out a few guys waiting inside. Thanks, brother," Ron said with a fist bump to his friend.

"The life you save may be your own," Link said with a chuckle.

"We cleared the house. Room to room, typical close-quarter combat," Red said. "Have you trained her on that yet?" he asked Axe.

"Haven't had time, though we've started through some obstacles on the range," Axe said.

"Good. Anyway, Haley, we get to the second floor," Thor said, laughing. "We're clearing rooms, shooting bad guys. Most of them were outside on the patio and decks to shoot at the helicopters and got clobbered by the big guns, but there were a few stragglers, including one guy…"

"We figure he was showering when the shooting started, then dropped into the tub for protection," Ronbo continued. "He's still wet —he didn't even reach up to turn the water off. He's drunk and pissed at us."

"Imagine!" Thor said.

"We get to the closed door of the bathroom, moving slow and quiet, though we had been shooting the hell out of people in the nearby rooms a few seconds before," Axe said.

"The door flies open," Thor said, but he was laughing so hard he couldn't continue.

Ron picked up the story. "And there's this naked guy, dripping wet, hair plastered to his head, holding an old-fashioned straight razor out and yelling like a maniac—some kind of war cry. He runs toward us. It was such a weird, funny sight I almost couldn't kill him."

"But you did, right?" Haley asked.

"Bet your ass. He was going after my guys. Shot him right between the eyes."

"So anyway," Red continued, "those guys are on the second floor while we're clearing the first floor. We find the target right away, sitting in the kitchen."

4

THE SMILE

Alex "Axe" Southmark's Cabin
Rural Virginia

Haley was about to ask what the target was doing in the kitchen, but Link spoke first.

"Don't tell her about the kitchen yet," Link said. "So we cleared the house, the garage. Eventually, the guards were all dead."

"They knew there was nowhere to go. It was win or die trying," Thor added.

"Only two people were alive, besides us," Ronbo said.

Red spoke quietly, his eyes on Axe. "We had them cornered in the kitchen. A standoff."

"We met up there and saw them," Ronbo continued. "The drug guy turned money launderer… and his wife."

At the mention of the woman, the men again went silent.

"Come on, guys, don't be creepy," Haley told them. "So she was attractive. You're acting like she was some kind of goddess."

One by one, they nodded thoughtfully. "Goddess, yes," Red said quietly. "I never thought of describing her that way, but it fits."

"Link, come on," Haley said. Out of all the men, she trusted him not to exaggerate. "Tell it straight."

"Haley," he said in his deep, methodical way. "This woman... Picture the most beautiful woman you've ever seen. One of those Roman statues? Or a supermodel? But combined with a puma. Her skin was dark. Just perfect. Thick, long black hair. Deep, soulful eyes. Perfect lips." He paused, struggling to describe the woman. "But it wasn't just her looks. We're not creeps. There was more to her. She... she had this air about her. An energy."

"It crackled," Thor blurted out. The others looked at him, and Haley knew this wasn't a usual part of the story but a new line, spoken from the heart.

"Okay, so she was what? Stunning?" she asked after several seconds without the men speaking.

More time passed as they remembered and considered her question.

"Captivating," Red whispered. The men nodded as one.

They aren't acting or putting me on, she thought. *They remember her so well, all the same way, like it was yesterday.*

Axe cleared his throat. "They're in this massive kitchen, all modern stainless steel in the middle of the jungle. It must have cost a fortune to bring in the marble floors and granite countertops. But they're sitting on these stools at the kitchen island like we hadn't just annihilated their entire army." He shook his head.

"Except she's holding his hand, as calm and composed as ever," Red explained.

"The dude, on the other hand, is waving a gun around, pointing it at his head, then at us, and back at his head," Axe told her.

"But never at her," Thor said.

"No, never at her. Then she whispers to him, and he starts sobbing," Ron said.

They enjoyed telling the story, and Haley guessed the good part was close—the part Axe would be reluctant to tell.

"Axe rushes forward from behind the guy, out of his line of sight, and grabs the gun," Red said.

"He didn't put up a fight at all," Axe said, his voice quieter than before. "He practically handed it to me."

"I was right behind with the zip cuffs," Link said, the front stairs creaking under his weight.

They were all silent for another second. Haley waited, desperate to know what happened next, sucked into their story.

"Then she turned to Axe and smiled," Link whispered.

5

THE NIGHT

Alex "Axe" Southmark's Cabin
Rural Virginia

What was supposed to be a quick story had turned long and drawn out. The late afternoon sun was setting. It would be cold and dark soon. If the men didn't wrap this up, Haley thought, Axe would have to invite them back in and serve another meal.

But Haley didn't want it to end.

She opened her mouth to ask what happened next, but something made her stop.

Let it come. This isn't how they usually tell it. Tonight, they're reliving the memory.

In the failing light, Axe had a strange expression on his face—a combination of happiness, regret, and something she couldn't put her finger on. Then it hit her.

She's the one that got away.

Thor tried to hide his unhappiness, but she could hear it in his voice. "Out of all of us standing there, guns drawn, she turns to Axe. Her smile…" He faltered.

"It hit me hard," Axe admitted.

"So they're making eyes at each other," Red said, trying but failing to break the spell with a joke. "Link takes the guy, and I order a few of the others to search the house for the computers, ledgers, whatever we need. But she..." He stopped and glanced at Axe.

"She leaned close and started telling me where everything was," Axe continued in his quiet voice. "Laptops, passwords..."

"And the money," Link added.

"The money," the guys said together, shaking their heads at the memory.

"There was this huge hidden underground room filled with money, shrink-wrapped. Glorious sight," Ronbo told her, his eyes filled with wonder. "Pallets of it! Stacked two high with narrow walkways between the rows."

"Anyway," Red said, once again trying to break the spell of remembrance they'd fallen into, "we gather up the dude, the computers, and hard copies of the data. We call the helicopters back. Miraculously, both are still flying, though the one Axe and I were in is in bad shape: rattling—more than usual—and trailing smoke. The pilot radios he can pick us up, but no guarantees he can make it back over the pass, even without us. With us, he's pretty sure we all go down hard."

"First," Link said, "no one left behind."

"No one left behind," they said in unison.

"But the intel, the gear, and the target can't get left behind, either. The one helicopter can't take us all, and we can't risk anything critical in the second bird," Red says.

"Which is when the woman slowly reaches out and takes Axe's hand," Thor said, his voice heavy with emotion.

All these years later, and he's still jealous.

Axe had the same far-off look in his eyes from earlier.

"Long story short, she takes Axe and I to the garage," Thor said, his voice quiet. "We'd seen the car before, when we cleared the compound. Red and black. Sleek, low to the ground. We found out later it costs one-and-a-half million dollars. But it's one thing to see it..."

"And another thing to drive it," Axe said with a smile.

"We loaded the HVT into chopper 1, along with everyone else and the intel. The second chopper flew back empty," Red explained.

"But before it took off," Ronbo said with a huge grin, "we loaded a duffel bag of cash into the damaged bird. They could always push it out the door if the chopper struggled. We figured, why not try? Then we hauled more of the money out of the secret room and to the car. We stuffed the small trunk with the bills..."

"Then I got into the driver's seat," Axe said, "and Red got in the passenger seat. I'm still not sure who got the better deal."

"I'd have to say it was you, Axe, driving the car," she told him.

Red's smile had a touch of sadness. "You'd think, right? But the woman had to ride somewhere. No back seat," he added.

"She sat on your lap?" Haley asked.

"Without complaint," he said with a sigh. "But I got the impression she wanted me to drive so she could sit on Axe's lap."

"But we'd already started dumping bundles of hundred-dollar bills on top of them—ten thousand dollars per packet. We filled that car up —they could hardly move," Thor said.

Haley suspected he'd been happy the woman was on Red's lap and not Axe's.

"It felt like one of those play pits—with the colorful balls?—from when we were kids," Red said.

"Every time I shifted, hundreds of thousands of dollars moved," Axe said. "It's the closest I'll ever come to filling up a pool and swimming in money."

"She sat on my lap," Red said quietly, getting back to the woman, "but all her energy was focused on Axe. I could sense her trying to figure a way out of the situation so they could be together."

Axe and Red stopped for a moment, lost in thought.

"The road out of the jungle was very well maintained," Axe finally continued quietly, "and we flew down it. An incredible car. I felt like I was in a fighter jet."

"And we were going almost as fast as one," Red said. "The woman knew where every guard checkpoint was, how to flash the high beams to signal it was the dude out for a night drive like the ones he took from time to time, according to her."

"When they left in the car," Ronbo said, "Axe had his elbow out the open window, like he didn't have a care in the world, sitting with packets of hundred-dollar bills piled up around him, driving a stolen million-dollar car, racing down that narrow jungle road. We lifted off in the chopper, only a few minutes ahead of the extra guards coming to help long after the battle had been lost. And Axe almost beat us back to base!"

"That's an exaggeration," Axe said, but Haley wondered.

They stopped talking, and the night finished fading to black.

"That's it?" Haley asked. "What happened to the money? The guy? The woman? Did she warm up to you, Red, on the ride?"

Red snorted. "I tried to make a move, but like I said, she only had eyes for Axe. Isn't that right, my friend?"

Axe shrugged and stared into the night.

"Back at base," Link rumbled, "we turned over the target, along with the intel. Then we carried the duffel bag into a room, counted the money together, and logged it in. We all stripped down to our briefs, turned out our pockets, and emptied our gear pouches. Although we trusted each other, we had to be sure. None of us wanted to wonder if anyone had sticky fingers, you know?"

"With fresh clothes on, we met Axe and Red at the gate to the base, so they got in okay," Thor said.

They met him at the car so they could see the woman again.

"We did the same with the money in the car—counted it together, logged it in, and Axe and Red stripped down, too," Link said. "No doubts—we were all clean."

"What about the woman? What happened to her?"

The question hung in the air, ignored.

"We got a commendation for the operation," Ronbo said with pride. "The authorities scooped up people left and right, shut down drug labs, froze bank accounts... the works. We put a huge dent in the drug and money-laundering operations—set them back years."

"And the money was a bonus. Not for us, you understand," Thor joked, his jealously gone for the moment. "We liberated fifty-seven million dollars. Though we had to torch the rest—in the house. There might have been a billion dollars there." He shook his head with regret.

"That's it," Red said, still quiet. "Operation Dark Moon."

It certainly wasn't one of their more boisterous stories. No one fell out of a helicopter. But Haley enjoyed hearing more about their exploits and life in the field. *One day soon, I'll have more stories to tell —and Axe and I might have a team like this one.*

They finally said their goodbyes with handshakes and bear hugs, thanking Axe for his hospitality—and making Haley once more feel like a part of the group—then drove off in their trucks.

These men lived in the darkness, awake all night, sleeping during the day. Tonight, they would read, work out, spend time with family and friends, and relax until it was time to gear up once more—for training or for combat.

Always either saving the world or preparing to.

ONE CRAZY NIGHT

Alex "Axe" Southmark's Cabin
Rural Virginia

Haley stood next to Axe on the porch, watching the last of the taillights disappear down the gravel driveway. The night had gotten cold. They'd been out longer than she'd expected, but she didn't want to go inside, or home, until she heard the end of the story.

"Are you going to tell me or not?" she asked quietly, her breath fogging in the cold air.

Axe sighed next to her. "Not much to tell, really."

"Seriously? It's me, Axe. Give."

He stuck his hands in his pockets and leaned against the pillar holding up the roof over the porch. She did the same on the other side of the stairs. No lights were on inside, but there was just enough starlight to see his face in the darkness. He looked... not exactly sad, but...

Wistful.

"She had a lot of information for the intel nerds and was happy to provide it in exchange for... something. I don't know the details, but they released her eventually."

"And?"

"We were back in Iraq by then, running and gunning every night. Capturing or killing bad guys, trying to win the war."

"You never saw her again?"

Axe shook his head in the darkness.

"That's it? No letters or phone calls, no crazy night together in Miami, or Bogotá, or wherever?"

Axe chuckled and shook his head again. "I didn't realize you were such a romantic."

"Neither did I," she admitted.

This has to be the one of the saddest stories I've ever heard.

They stood on the porch, each lost in thought. Eventually, Axe broke the silence. "I've loved a few things in my life. My family, to start. My country. My Higher Power. The Teams, and my teammates, which includes you. But a connection like I felt with—" He stopped, not saying her name. "It hit me hard, and I thought the feeling would never come again. But you sent me to Montauk on our first mission together. I almost got myself killed, but I met Connie in the helicopter on the way to the hospital. I had the same feeling when I saw her as that night years ago in the jungle. An instant connection." He looked at her with a grateful smile, his wistfulness gone. "So thanks, partner."

Axe gave her the same bear hug he'd given the guys.

She didn't know what to say, so she hugged him back and said, "You're welcome."

"Don't worry, you'll find the one for you," he whispered, reading her mind.

She stepped back and shook her head. "How? All I do is bury my head in the threats facing the country and go into the field to…" She didn't want to say it.

"To kill people. I get it. It's what we do. But I found love. Connie is perfect for me; she understands. Your guy will be the one who accepts that the operation will always come first." He laughed. "As long as he's not a bad guy you have to kill, you're fine."

Now that would be a problem.

They headed back inside. She gathered up her things, including the boxing gloves Axe had given her, and said goodbye. Then she headed home, still wondering how, when, and where she'd meet the man for her.

———

———

OPERATION SWING TIME

1

THE HOTEL GRAND LAGOON

The gathering in this story takes place immediately *before* the last chapter of *A Team of Three*.

The Hotel Grand Lagoon
Key Largo, Florida

Axe set the pace as they started. Not easy—this was a training run, after all—but not hard. Yet. He could certainly have a conversation at this pace. Which was a mistake, because his medium pace was easy for Haley. She was more than twenty years younger than he was, and no matter how hard he worked out, how much he stuck to his nutrition plan, and how few beers he limited himself to, she would forever be faster than him.

Growing old isn't for wimps, he thought.

The sun was rising to their left as they ran down the beach from the resort hotel where they were staying. Axe's girlfriend, Connie, and Haley's boyfriend, Derek, were likely meeting for coffee right now. Neither liked to exercise first thing in the morning.

It's not a choice for Haley and me. Life is constant, ongoing training.

Each day was either a training day or a mission day. There was no time off—not if they wanted to be fast and strong enough to survive the next operation.

At this hour, there was no one else on the beach. It was barely light enough to see. When the sun rose, the early birds would come out to walk or swim in the Gulf. But for now, they had what seemed like the entire Florida Keys to themselves.

The easy pace—for Haley—provided the opportunity she needed to chat, though he'd rather enjoy the quiet of the morning.

"Tell me about some of your earlier missions," she told him, her long legs nearly matching his strides. She had her hair up in a high ponytail, which disguised her beauty somewhat. It would come in handy in a while when they encountered the first walkers on the beach. Both men and women would stare as she ran by, even with her luxurious blond hair pulled back severely. Another reason they ran before dawn.

I've created a monster, telling her the stories of the old days on the Teams.

Warriors had several ways to process the powerful emotions they dealt with on the battlefield. Day to day, Axe and his old teammates defaulted to humor, using dark comedy to manage stress and stay sane.

Another tool was the telling of tales. "Never let the truth stand in the way of a good story," was their mantra, though rarely did anyone have to exaggerate. They'd "been there and done that," as the other saying went.

Axe and his former Team, including Red, Thor, Link, and Ronbo, had introduced Haley to the tradition to help her work through the experiences of her first few missions. Killing people never came easy —and shouldn't—but Haley hadn't been prepared for the violence she'd faced. Axe's solution had been to invite Haley and his buddies over to his cabin in the Virginia woods, drink beer, tell stories, bond, and let shit go.

Since then, Haley had occasionally pestered him for more. But he preferred telling the old tales in a group setting, reliving the adventures with the others who had been there.

Still, they're good stories that need to be told. And unfortunately, several of my first Team aren't around anymore, so why not?

It would keep their memories alive—and transfer the stories into the mind of the next generation. For whether Haley realized it or not, she was the future.

"You heard about Operation Rapid Revenge."

"That poor goat," she mumbled. A goat had broken loose during a firefight and dashed into a minefield, revealing the surprise the enemy had planned for the SEAL Team.

"That 'poor goat' saved our lives," he reminded her.

"I get it. That was your first op, right?"

"Yes."

"So tell me about the second one."

Axe thought back, trying to recall the next operation. After so many years, all those nights of recon, assaults, and missions, they blended together.

"The next several, best I can remember, were typical missions. I was the new guy. While I did well on the first op, I didn't have the experience the others had. So I watched and learned."

Axe saw the disappointed look on her face.

"Not what you wanted to hear?" he asked.

"No, I get it. Not every mission warrants a story."

"Exactly."

Hell, why not throw the kid a bone?

"There was one, in the first few months," he said, thinking back.

"Let's hear it."

She knew enough by now not to ask him where it happened. He wouldn't tell her. Rules were rules.

He ran on for a bit, silent, just to mess with her. But when she finally turned and glared at him, he chuckled and started the story. "Okay. So no shit, there I was…"

2

BUILDING 2

Many Years Earlier
A City in the Middle East

Axe followed the line of men—his Team—as they silently slipped through the sleeping city. The capture-or-kill mission would be unique in some ways, certainly, but he'd now been on enough missions to feel like he had a handle on the process.

We get in, get the bad guy, and get out.

After an uneventful hike through the dark city streets, they arrived at the target. There were four six-story apartment buildings in a group. One of them housed the man they were to capture, according to a paid informant.

The signal came to halt. Axe crouched near the trunk of a beat-up old car, spinning to cover the street they had advanced up. Trouble could come from any direction. If people had noticed them passing, an attack from the rear was entirely possible. It was Axe's job to watch for it.

The dusty, trash-strewn street glowed green in his night vision goggles.

The wait seemed endless. Behind him, the four apartment buildings loomed. Axe was shielded from view, but the cheaply made car wouldn't stop a bullet from any of the dozens of windows overlooking the position.

I may not know a lot, but this isn't the place to stop for any length of time.

His role as the new guy, though, didn't allow for him to get on the radio and ask what the hell the holdup was.

I'm sure someone in front is asking that question right now.

A tap came on his shoulder from the SEAL behind him. The man gestured for him to head to the front of the column, staying low.

Axe bent at the waist and hurried forward.

Two other SEALS—"Tiger" and "Rain Man"—gathered next to JT, the unit's best sniper, and their team lead, call sign "Duke."

"Axe, go with JT and these guys up that building," Duke said, pointing to the first apartment building on the right. "You're overwatch."

A second later, they were off.

The lock on the building's front door was broken and looked like it had been for years, which allowed them to slip inside easily. They knew the rough layout. The buildings were identical, not that finding the stairs next to the non-working elevator in the middle of the run-down lobby would have been difficult.

Axe brought up the rear again. JT was in the middle, his long gun strapped to his back and M4 ready for any close-quarter combat that would be required for them to get into position.

The intel claimed the four-building complex was friendly to Americans, aside from the bad element in one of building 2's apartments.

The intel is always wrong, Axe thought.

The saying had been mumbled, almost like a prayer, by the entire group during the briefing earlier. It always annoyed the intel geeks, which was half the fun.

But they also said it because it was true—which the intel geeks knew and couldn't refute. Those guys had a tough, albeit safer, gig than the front-line warriors. With limited resources and unreliable human sources, they were doing the best they could—which was actually damn good, all things considered.

But it paid to take the intelligence with a grain of salt.

They ascended the stairs softly but quickly, stepping over yet more trash. *Why don't people in this country pick up after themselves?* It wasn't like anyone came along and did it for them. No, the people seemed fine with refuse everywhere.

A metal door at the top of the stairs posed no problems, either. The lock was gone, leaving a hole where a deadbolt had once been.

They cleared the roof, ensuring no one slept outside. In many months, the heat, even at night, was too oppressive to sleep indoors. And with power intermittent, people would have been fighting for space on the roof if the weather had been any warmer. Thankfully, it hadn't turned that hot yet.

While JT set up away from the edge of the flat roof, at an angle to what they believed was the correct bad-guy apartment, Axe had the job of watching the door for unwanted visitors and protecting JT—and the others, who had the more enviable job of covering the courtyard between the apartments and the streets leading to it.

One of these days there will be a new new guy, and I won't get the boring shit duties.

Still, "watching their six" was an essential job, and he'd proven himself a few weeks earlier. He'd started to make a name for himself as one to stay cool and clever under fire when he'd led the Team through the minefield—after the goat exploded.

Nothing was happening yet, so Axe risked a question to JT, who lay near him, prone behind the sniper rifle. The long gun was overkill at such close ranges—any SEAL could have killed a man inside the three other apartment buildings near them with an M4. But JT's shooting skills were legendary. If he wanted to use the sniper rifle, no one would question it.

"What was the holdup down there?" Axe asked in a very soft whisper.

"Discussion about which one is actually building 2," JT answered softly, the gun never wavering from the target.

Axe knew they were both thinking the same thing yet again.

The intelligence is always wrong.

3

THE BEACH

Key Largo, Florida

"I take exception to that slogan," Haley said as they continued their run.

Axe took her words to heart. *She sounds like she's joking... but she isn't,* he thought.

"Remember," Axe said, "this was long before you and your intelligence analysis." He did the math in his head.

She was about five years old then.

Suddenly, he felt ancient.

No. Experienced, not old.

At least, that's what he kept telling himself.

"The men and women of the intelligence division did an amazing job—we couldn't have succeeded without them."

"But...?"

"But there was a lot of confusion."

"What happened in this case?" Haley asked.

"Our people were spot on. The problem wasn't the intelligence. It was the informant. We never found out if it was a setup or if the guy really didn't know which building was which."

"What's your hunch?"

Her questions surprised him. How did she know he'd put more thought into it than necessary—or healthy?

She's better at reading my face—or my mind.

"My hunch is that the bad guys routinely changed around the big numbers labeling the buildings to purposefully confuse outsiders. They had to know we were going to hit them eventually. Swapping the numbers was a form of insurance."

"So your Team hit the wrong building? Or was the whole thing a trap?"

She's learning...

4

THE TRAP

Many Years Earlier
A City in the Middle East

There was minimal talking over the radio, just enough to communicate effectively where the other four men of the Team were. They had started up the stairwell of the building directly across from Axe, JT, and the other two SEALs.

So far, so good.

But something felt off.

The old guys say, "Always trust your gut."

"You feel it?" he whispered to JT. The sniper had been friendly, welcoming Axe and encouraging his dream of going to sniper training school after he had more combat experience. "My instincts are screaming at me."

"Yep," JT whispered matter-of-factly. He didn't seem bothered in the least.

Well... damn. Now what?

"Shouldn't we, I don't know, do something?"

"What do you want to do?"

Good question.

Axe glanced around. He was on the roof of a four-story apartment building in the middle of a foreign city filled with people who welcomed them—and many who didn't.

The surrounding area was supposed to be relatively friendly, but you never knew. All they had was each other, their weapons, and their experience. Which, in Axe's case, wasn't much.

"Check the perimeter?"

"Is that a question?"

The SEALs weren't big on orders—or handholding.

Axe took a breath, finding his backbone. "No. I'm checking the door first, then the perimeter."

"Copy."

Crouched low, Axe moved as he'd been taught.

Slow is smooth, and smooth is fast.

As he neared the door to the stairwell, he got a tingly feeling on both arms. He couldn't see or hear anyone, but it didn't matter.

Trouble. There are people in the stairwell.

He whispered into the sensitive mic at the corner of his mouth. "People coming up the stairs of building 1."

"Copy," came the response from JT. He stayed where he was, but Tiger and Rain Man shifted their positions. They still covered their sectors but could swing to back him up if needed.

Axe had closed the metal door behind him when they'd arrived at the roof. He put the NVGs near the deadbolt hole and looked through. A man with an AK appeared on the landing and stalked toward the door. Behind him, another man moved up the stairs, with a third man behind him. They were military age and armed—which didn't mean much in this country. It seemed like everyone had an AK.

The rules of engagement are clear. I can engage the enemy in the bad guy's apartment, or anyone shooting at me, but I can't just open fire at anyone, even if they have a weapon.

Although unlikely, the men could be the building's hired security guards coming to find the intruders on the roof.

How solid is this door?

He held his left hand out, using gestures to communicate with his Team. At least one of the men on the roof would have eyes on him.

The assumption was confirmed an instant later. "Axe indicates we're about to have company," Tiger said over the radio. "Three tangos, possibly more."

Duke, their team lead in building 2, came on the radio an instant later. "We're thirty seconds away from our target. Hold them off silently until you hear our shots if possible."

Next to the door and ready to call out a challenge to see if the men on the stairs would open fire on him, Axe frowned.

Way to make it harder, Duke.

He slung his M4, drew the razor-sharp knife hanging upside down from its sheath on his plate carrier, and prepared himself.

The only easy day was yesterday.

5

PUSH-UPS

Key Largo, Florida

They had reached the end of the hard-packed sandy beach as Axe told his story. Instead of turning around right away, Axe stopped, dropped, and started push-ups. Haley joined him with a grimace.

This is where I make it look easy and she struggles, unlike the running, Axe thought.

Every day, he did set after set of push-ups. They were an easy way to stay fit and burn off excess energy.

"You were relatively new, right?" Haley asked, doing one push-up for every two of his.

"Yes."

I know where she's going with this.

"And no," he added, "I had never killed anyone with my knife. I'd been trained, of course, and had practiced over and over again. But…"

"Yeah," Haley said quietly, surely remembering several months before, when she'd killed with a knife. "It feels much different than you think it will." She paused. "Almost… intimate."

He didn't bother to answer her. He just kept pumping out the push-ups, counting hers instead of his own. When she reached twenty-five, he finished his last one and started running back the way they had come, pushing it a little harder than before, his mind going back to that night.

6

THE DOOR

Many Years Earlier
A City in the Middle East

Axe stood near the door to the roof, desperate for a plan.

I have to follow the ROE and not kill the first guy right away, but I have to also keep him and his buddies quiet for the next thirty seconds.

How the hell was he supposed to do that?

Shit.

He secured his knife back into its sheath and flattened himself against the wall next to the door.

Time to test all that hand-to-hand combat they taught us.

Shuffling came from the other side of the door.

They're moving into position.

The door didn't move.

Metal hit the railing in the stairwell. Axe wouldn't have heard it if he hadn't been standing where he was. On the stairs, all movement immediately stopped.

They're holding to see if we heard them—and there are more than three men.

He counted in his head. The enemy's hesitancy played to his advantage.

Twenty seconds left. Maybe—

He didn't get any further. The door flew open and the first man stepped through, his AK held at waist level like a Wild West gunslinger with a shotgun instead of a man who understood the importance of aiming a rifle—even a fully automatic one.

Axe struck him in the throat, likely breaking his larynx—if he'd done it correctly. Just in case he hadn't, he followed up with a strike to the man's nose, shattering it.

Good luck breathing, buddy.

Then he grabbed the man's weapon, tore it from his grasp, and used it to push him back inside, onto the stairwell's landing.

When in doubt, create confusion.

"Help," he quietly cried in the local language on behalf of the man, who wouldn't ever speak again.

The assault of the roof faltered before it really began. Axe, crouched and hidden by the darkness and the smaller, thinner man's body, gently pushed the enemy back farther, against the next man in line, choking out another "help" as he did.

Fifteen seconds.

He nudged the man once more, which caused the second one to take his comrade's weight even as he had to step back into the next man—standing at the top of the stairs.

The second man whispered something, but Axe didn't catch it. He only knew a few words in the language. But with the injured man struggling to breathe, and the attack stopped for the moment, he didn't have to worry.

Seconds passed while the man holding his injured friend tried to make sense of the situation. There were others waiting on the stairs, all armed with AKs, but none with the precious night vision goggles that gave the SEALs an enormous advantage.

They can't see me or what's going on.

All were tightly packed, ready to charge up the last few steps to the roof.

Five seconds.

The opportunity in front of him was too good to pass up.

Four, three...

He raised his foot, planted his big boot on the gasping man's stomach, and pushed with all his strength.

For a second, nothing happened. Then the men toppled back into the man on the next lower step... who took their weight and fell back into the next man... and so on down the stairs.

The men toppled like dominos in the dark.

Two, one...

From the other building, the low boom of a breaching charge carried across the quiet courtyard.

7

DAWN

Key Largo, Florida

It was harder to tell the story running fast, but Axe got it out piece by piece. He slowed, then stopped. The sun was coming up.

Haley groaned but dropped onto the hard sand next to him for more push-ups. "So no knife?" she asked as she lowered herself to the ground.

"Not that day," Axe said.

He did the push-ups slower than usual, which allowed him to catch his breath.

"Was that it? Duke and company got the bad guy, you guys shot up the ones in the stairwell, and everyone exfilled home in time for ice cream and the Late Show?"

"Not exactly."

8

SWING TIME

Many Years Earlier
A City in the Middle East

Heavy gunfire from the other building—not all of it from his fellow SEALs' M4s—told Axe the mission wasn't going as planned.

"Heavy contact," Duke said, his voice calm. He could have been commenting on a lovely day at the beach.

"There's nobody in the courtyard—you're clear there. But I don't have a shot through any windows, sorry," JT said.

"Team 2, can you guys get over here and back us up?"

Axe waited a moment for JT or one of the other guys to speak up, then realized it was up to him.

I'm the one with the door intel, so I guess it's my call.

The men on the stairs were sorting themselves out and answering questions from others who called up from farther down.

"Our stairwell has a lot of tangos," he said over the radio. He had three grenades and plenty of ammo. Holding them off would be possible for a while, but assaulting down through them would be difficult and very risky.

His eyes swept the roof. He considered prying the door from its hinges—they could use it as a shield—but every landing they made it to might have more men waiting for them.

They carried rope and could rappel to the ground. It would take time to rig, but it was probably their best bet.

"We have contact from the floor above us and below!" Duke said. His voice was less calm.

For his voice to sound like that, things are dicey.

Axe's eyes fell on the thick clump of wires connecting the buildings. He didn't know if they were for telephones, electricity, or the ever-present satellite dishes, but there were dozens of wires forming a rope thicker than his forearm. "JT, cover them. You two," he called to the more senior men watching their sectors, "test out that hunk of cables. See if it will take your weight. We can use it to get to the roof and assault down to our guys from above. The tangos will never see us coming."

For a long moment, neither man moved. Axe had no authority to order them around, but the way the SEAL Teams worked, anyone could throw out an idea. If it solved the problem, it was embraced, even if it came from the new guy. The SEAL Ethos was clear. One section contained the line, "In the absence of orders, I will take charge, lead my teammates and accomplish the mission."

Rain Man finally rushed over and gave the cords a hard yank. They held. He slung his rifle, grabbed the mess of wires again, and inched his way off the roof, letting the tangled rope of wires take his weight. When he didn't plummet to the ground, he swung his legs up, hooked his ankles over the wires, and pulled himself quickly toward the other building.

Just like in BUD/S, Axe thought, still guarding the door. They'd run the obstacle course hundreds of times, navigating a thick rope between two points, backs to the ground as they pulled themselves across.

Tiger covered him while JT kept the overwatch.

It was at that moment the men in the stairwell got their act together. A burst of AK fire slammed into the metal door but didn't penetrate.

Thanks for the warning, guys—and the go-ahead to fight back.

He pulled the pin on a grenade, opened the door a few inches, tossed the grenade into the stairwell, and ducked.

The explosion shook the roof but only stopped the assault for a few seconds. Gunfire fire came from farther down the stairs. It didn't threaten Axe, but it proved there were plenty of other enemy combatants on their way.

Rain Man was across safely and positioned to cover the door to the roof on building 2.

Tiger lowered himself onto the cables, swung his legs up as Rain Man had—as they'd all been taught—and started across.

Despite the sporadic gunfire from the stairs, Axe prepared his next grenade.

Time for more party favors.

Axe hugged the ground before cracking the door again. He tossed a second grenade. Bullets from AK fire hit the door where his head would have been had he not been gone low.

The explosion silenced the AK fire, but more angry shouting came up the stairwell.

He only had one grenade left.

The intensity of fire from the other building picked up. His brothers were in trouble.

"JT, go!" Tiger wasn't all the way across, but there wasn't much time—for them… or the men in the other building.

While the enemy on the stairs dealt with the carnage he'd inflicted, Axe opened the door and fired a burst to slow them down.

Let them think I'm out of grenades.

Answering AK fire forced him to close the door and cover again—but it bought him a few extra seconds.

The enemy finally got itself together again and tried a new approach. The AK fire picked up—a steady barrage of bullets hitting the door and the frame around it, top to bottom.

Guess they finally figured out the concept of covering fire.

The enemy would have a few men on the landing where the stairs switched direction, turning back on themselves before descending to the floor below. They were firing while one or more people came in under the bullets to kill him.

JT had made it to the middle of the span between the buildings. It was time to go.

Can the wires support both of us?

He cracked the door. Bullets pinged inches from his face, but he lobbed the last grenade in and rolled away from danger before leaping to his feet and running toward the corner of the building.

JT must have seen him and worried about the weight of both of them on the wire, because he moved even faster.

The grenade blew behind him as Axe leaped off the building, grabbing the cables several feet from the edge as he soared through the air.

The sudden weight on the cables—combined with JT's body still hanging from them—caused the mess of wires to separate from however they were being held in place against the building.

Axe plummeted, arcing through the air like a man on a vine in the jungle.

The wires were pulled from the varying directions they ran, slowing his swing.

Building 2 loomed in front of him, clear as daylight in the NVGs. He hit the wall, more gently than he expected but still enough to jar him and make him bounce away.

The wires separated, no longer in a strand. Instead, they looked like a spider web spreading to the various apartments behind him as he twisted and hit the wall a second time.

Alive and unharmed, his only thought was for JT on the wire above him. When he looked up, he wasn't there.

No. Oh, God, no.

"JT?" Axe looked down, praying he wouldn't see the man's broken, lifeless body splattered on the ground below.

"I'm safe, you crazy asshole," came the instant response over the radio. "I made it as you did your monkey impression." He stopped talking and started shooting, the distinctive sound of his suppressed sniper rifle coming over the radio.

He's picking off the tangos coming through the door of building 1.

"I've got the roof," JT said. "Rain Man and Tiger are heading down the stairs."

"Copy," Axe said. He was to the left and a few feet below a tiny third-floor balcony. He could lower himself down to the matching balcony of the apartment on the second floor, but he'd be on the same level as his brothers.

He pulled himself up and grabbed the edge of the balcony.

"Contact stairwell, level 5," Tiger called.

Damn, we've got tangos everywhere.

Axe pulled himself onto the balcony, broke open the door, and ran past two figures huddled in the far corner of the room. Then he stealthily made his way out of the frightened couple's apartment, into the deserted hallway, and to the door to the stairs. "Friendly on the third floor," he whispered into the radio. "Who needs the most help?"

"We're fine for the moment," Tiger said.

"Axe, assault to us from above!" Duke called.

"Copy. Moving."

The M4 fire from below slacked off, directed more at the enemy on the stairs below Duke than in Axe's direction.

Stealth or speed?

He could probably sneak up behind the men and take them out one by one with his knife. It would be slower and quieter—and perhaps a little safer for him. But every second in the firefight allowed other bad guys to get into position, making their exfil more dangerous.

Stealth now, then speed.

He opened the door to the stairwell slowly. Men lined the stairs, waiting their turn to fire. A few pointed their AKs over the railing and fired down on his brothers, likely hitting nothing, but putting bullets downrange.

The man nearest him turned and tried to figure out who was coming through the door.

Surprise, asshole.

Axe shot him in the face, then raked the line of enemy. They fell.

He put more bullets into each man as he rushed down the stairs, killing the next batch of fighters.

In seconds, it was done.

"Clear above the second floor," Axe said as he rushed back up the stairs, careful to not slip on the rapidly spreading blood. "Coming up. Tiger, hold your fire for a second."

"Copy, Ape Man," Tiger said.

9

THE SECRET

Key Largo, Florida

Axe hoped he wouldn't regret telling Haley the story.

She laughed as they continued to run back toward the hotel. "Ape Man? I love it. Can I—"

"No," Axe said. "Absolutely not. You can't call me that. 'Papa' is bad enough." The call sign his former Team had given him when he'd joined them on a mission—poking fun at what they had called his "advancing years"—hit a little too close to home.

"Anyway, I killed the guys threatening Tiger, Rain Man, and JT from below, then we all joined Duke, overwhelmed the rest of the enemy, killed the target, and got the hell out of there. Mission accomplished."

They ran on. Axe picked up the pace more as he thought about those years. *As hard as I've worked to stay in shape, I doubt I could pull off that stunt today.*

Not that he wouldn't try if needed, though.

"Can I confide in you, Blondie?" Axe asked, using her call sign to show this was something to take seriously.

"Always," she said, one-hundred percent serious. He was happy to see the punishing pace he had set was finally causing her to breathe heavier.

"The guys gave me credit for the swing, like I had planned it out. But it was all luck. I meant to hand-over-hand it onto building 2's roof like the other guys had."

Haley contemplated his admission. "They couldn't have all thought you did it on purpose."

"Probably not, but I never admitted the truth. Though, to my credit, I never claimed it was my plan, either."

"Your secret is safe with me," Haley said.

Axe smiled. "You know what my dad always used to say? 'Better lucky than good.'"

"But we prefer to be both."

"Yes, we do."

"So you had the right building all along?"

"Yes, but not because of the intel. Duke figured it out somehow. He was a great guy."

"Was?"

"Is. He's still around. Retired. I'll have to look him up." He could take Haley, and she could hear more stories.

They finally slowed, both panting, as they neared the resort.

When they had their breath back, Haley asked, "How long did they call you Ape Man?"

Axe laughed. "It felt like forever! But I got 'Axe' back, eventually."

"How?"

He stared out at the waters of the Gulf of Mexico, remembering the feel of the axe in his blood-covered hands. "Long story," he said, shaking his head. "Let's go eat." *One story is enough for today.*

With that, they walked off the beach and onto the resort's pathway leading to the dining room. Connie and Derek were waiting.

OPERATION END RUN

1

THE HOTEL GRAND LAGOON

The gathering in this story takes place immediately *after* the ending of *A Team of Three.*

The Hotel Grand Lagoon
Key Largo, Florida

The chilly late-evening breeze off the water had already sent the other resort guests, along with Connie, Senator Woodran—Barbara—and Derek back to their rooms. Only Axe, Haley, and Nalen remained. They sat in contented silence, ignoring the cold after scooting their wooden Adirondack-style chairs closer to the hotel's gas fire pit near the beach.

It was their last night at the resort. Tomorrow, Axe and Derek would drive north to home, transporting Haley's weapons so she could fly directly back to work without any hassle, having finally agreed to return to her old job at the Central Analysis Group.

"I hate to sound like a little kid..." Haley said, trailing off and brushing her long blond hair from her face as the breeze grabbed it.

"But you want a bedtime story," Axe said.

Haley nodded.

Why not? Axe thought. *Storytelling never gets old—especially around friends.*

By this point, though, the three of them were much more than friends. They had fought and risked their lives together. Defended each other. Laughed, cried, and shared the good and the bad. It had created a bond deeper than friends. They knew more about what each other thought and felt than the tightest family or closest couples.

To call us a band of brothers—and a sister—doesn't come close to capturing the connection.

"You know how parents give their kids a five-minute warning before they have to leave the playground, go to bed, or whatever?" Axe asked Haley. "This is your heads-up. At some point very soon, it'll be your turn to tell a tale."

Haley's shock didn't surprise Axe.

She doesn't realize how much she's done and accomplished.

"What story can I tell that you haven't heard?" she countered.

"True," he admitted. "Tonight, in this company, you can listen. Like I said, it's your warning. But next time we're in a group of warriors we trust, you're up."

From the look on her face, Axe guessed the thought scared her more than facing down an overwhelming force of the enemy, which they'd done on more than one occasion.

"Only if you tell me how you got your Team to stop calling you Ape Man," she said.

"Ape Man?" Nalen said. "That was your call sign?"

Axe glared playfully—mostly—across the fire at Haley. "Long story, Admiral," Axe said to Nalen with a sigh. "For another night, now that 'Comet' has blabbed."

"Comet?" Haley asked. Then she got it—Haley's comet. "No," she said, shaking her head. "Blondie makes more sense."

"What, you don't want to be named after one of Santa's reindeer?" Axe joked.

"If we're going to change her call sign, it would be fitting to use something about her intelligence," Nalen said thoughtfully.

"Megamind? Brainiac?" Axe suggested.

"Genius?"

"Guys," Haley growled, clearly not enjoying the direction the conversation had gone.

"No, it should start with an 'H,'" Nalen said. "That's what's bothered me about 'Blondie' from the start."

"And it's too descriptive," Axe said. "No one knows from looking at me that I'm Axe. But with her…"

"True," Nalen agreed. "'Blondie' is operationally risky."

"'H'… Houston? Hotshot?" Axe asked.

"Hotshot's not terrible."

"Gentlemen, seriously, can we get back to Ape Man's story?"

Axe paused for a second, sighed theatrically, and adjusted himself on the chair, pretending to prepare himself for the story. Then he looked at Nalen again and said, "What about 'Highbrow'? No," he said a second later. "Man, 'H' words are hard, aren't they, Hammer?"

Haley rolled her eyes.

"We might have to stick with 'Comet' for now," Nalen said after several seconds of thinking.

"Or Blondie," Haley said. "Blondie has a nice ring to it." She turned to Axe. "So—no shit, there you were…" she prompted.

Axe chuckled, then stared into the fire, his humor fading as he remembered.

"So no shit, there I was," he said quietly, as his thoughts took him to the day he earned back his call sign.

2

THE TARGET

The Hotel Grand Lagoon
Key Largo, Florida

"I can't tell you where I was, of course," Axe began. "We were running and gunning every night, taking down bad guys. We did well, but no matter how hard we worked, there were always more to catch."

"I remember those days," Nalen said. "From the command side, we hated it. It was like playing Whac-A-Mole with the enemy."

"I bet you'll remember the mission," Axe said to Nalen. "We caught a break—an enemy leader wanted to give himself up, tell his story, spill all the secrets."

"I remember," Nalen said, shaking his head. "And all he wanted in exchange was a few million dollars and a new life of leisure in a tranquil western European county."

"You did things like that?" Haley asked.

Nalen shrugged. "We were hungry for an edge. Besides, what's a few million if it spared lives and brought the country closer to peace?"

Many Years Earlier
The Middle East

"The brass claim he's holed up in a village," Duke, their team lead, explained as he led the mission brief. "It's relatively nearby, but there are several problems. One," he said, holding up a finger. "It's a no-go zone for helicopters—reports of tons of RPGs and a rumor of portable surface-to-air missiles. We'll be tasked with taking those out in the next few nights, by the way. Two," he said, ticking off the next finger. "It works better if the enemy doesn't know we have the guy. The intel he's willing to provide could break things wide open here—but as soon as they know he's gone over to our side, the rats will scatter. Plans will change. So if we want him, we go in and bring him out quiet-like. On foot."

Axe sat next to Tiger in the briefing room at the base, soaking it in. He was no longer the new guy, thank God. But he was still newish, so he kept his mouth shut and let his actions speak for him.

But Tiger could never resist a few comments, spoken quietly so only Axe could hear. "Total scam. Double-cross ambush bullshit," he muttered.

Duke stopped talking in the middle of his sentence.

Shit, Axe thought.

"You have something to add, Ape Man?" Duke called at them.

Damn it, Tiger!

Next to him, Tiger snorted his amusement while keeping a straight face.

"How fit is the target?" Axe asked.

"What the hell are you talking about?"

"Is he out of shape? Young, old? Can he run, or at least walk?"

Duke, a tough, extremely fit old-school SEAL, stood with his hands on his hips and glared at him. "If I could continue?"

Axe nodded and said, "Sorry."

"Thank you. Shut the hell up when I'm giving a briefing, Ape Man, and you'll learn all you need to know. Now, as I was saying, we're on foot for a few K. We'll take a chopper to here," he said, pointing at a map. "Civilian vehicles will be waiting for you, guarded by supposedly reliable locals on our side. Then we'll drive here," he said, pointing at a few scattered buildings along the main road through the area. "Four of us will walk in to secure the target. Four will stay with the vehicles. They'll be the quick reaction force if things go wrong."

He sent another glare Axe's way. "The target is middle-aged, slightly overweight, but can handle a few kilometers' walk—his claim, and our intel concurs." Duke looked around the briefing room at the gathered SEALs. "Questions so far? Ape Man, I trust the plan to this point meets with your approval?"

Axe nodded once.

Anything I say only gets me in deeper.

"Wonderful. Here's the rest." Duke continued the briefing, laying out an overview of the surrounding area, the routes they'd take to an extraction point, and contingency plans.

As he finished up, Duke moved to personnel. "Ape Man, since you're so concerned about the target's health, I'm subbing you in on the first team." Duke glared at Tiger. "And Tiger, you buddy up with Ape Man. The two of you can carry the target out if needed."

Axe and Tiger nodded.

"And yes," Duke continued, "tonight could very well be yet another in a long line of ambushes. But we have a solid plan, even if this is a lure to draw us in. If we're being set up, it just means we're going to be able to show the enemy what we're made of and take a bunch of them out. Fewer to hunt down and capture or kill."

The briefing finished up moments later.

"Sorry," Tiger muttered to Axe as the others stood up to prep for the night.

"About what? Getting us on the main team?" Axe asked. "You think I signed up to drive a truck and do escort duty, or hang back as a QRF? No way."

"Well, don't mess up and die tonight, all right? It would take me a day or two to get over sending you to your death," Tiger said, fighting back a smile.

"Deal."

They joined the others for a meal, equipment check, and some downtime before they launched the mission.

Tonight's going to be full of action. I can feel it.

3

THE AMBUSH

The Hotel Grand Lagoon
Key Largo, Florida

The breeze off the water had picked up. Haley shivered and scooted her chair around the fire pit to catch more of the warmth from the flames as the wind shifted.

I should have brought a warmer jacket, she thought.

"Let me guess," she said, rubbing her arms. "The intelligence was wrong."

Axe and Nalen both laughed.

"No," Nalen said.

"For once, the intelligence was solid," Axe conceded. "They thought it might be a trap, and they were right. But we go in no matter what. It could have been for real."

"When did they hit you? At the civilian vehicles?"

"No, they drew us in. The approach was fine. In fact, we were early, so instead of waiting until the agreed-upon time, we moved up the timeline."

Many Years Earlier
The Middle East

Axe watched his sector through NVGs as Duke spoke quietly nearby. "We're an hour early," Duke announced over the radio. His voice came through Axe's headphone and as a nearby whisper in the quiet night. "But we're not waiting around. The target should already be here, according to the intel geeks. So let's get him—quietly—and get out."

Smart. If it's an ambush, we might have the jump on them.

They snuck silently through the village to the target home, as quiet as ghosts. Near the door to the small mud hut, small pieces of firewood were stacked neatly. A stump served as a place to cut logs into kindling. An axe was embedded into the log.

Axe grabbed it.

No sense leaving a weapon lying around.

It wasn't much: a wooden handle, well worn. The blade looked sharp, though, and it had a good heft to it. More of a long hatchet, or a short axe. He wouldn't keep it, but when his gut told him to pick it up, he did. He slid it into a flap of his plate carrier and prepared to enter the small house, attached on both sides and the rear to other homes in the small, poor village.

Tiger lifted the latch of the front door and Axe slid in silently, clearing his area as Rain Man, the third SEAL along, followed him and cleared the other sector of the room. Duke and Tiger waited outside, covering their exfil.

It was a one-room home. Clean and neat. Mostly empty, except for a man sitting on a thin cushion on the floor, half asleep. He was chubby, dressed decently in the local custom, and unarmed. But he looked surprised to see Axe in the dim light shining through the two small front windows.

Axe raised a finger to his lips in the universal gesture for quiet. Then he moved his hand, encouraging the man to stand.

That's when his gut told him something was wrong. A second later, the call came over the radio.

"Movement out front," Duke said, his voice tighter than usual. "Let's go!"

Rain Man took the target by the arm to lead him outside. Axe brought up the rear.

Then the bullets started flying.

"Contact front," Tiger announced as if they needed it said. The clatter of first one, then two, then an overwhelming number of AKs mixed with the sound of Tiger and Duke's M4s.

"Two coming in. Move it back!"

An instant later, as Rain Man pulled the target to the rear corner of the small home, Tiger and Duke crashed through the door.

The gunfire slacked off for a moment as the enemy hesitated. But they must have gotten an order because more bullets turned on the house, shattering the windows. A few punched through the hardened straw and mud walls.

"They're everywhere. We're not getting out that way," Tiger announced.

They were trapped.

While Duke called on the QRF, ordering them to drive to the village, Tiger and Rain Man traded shots with the enemy through the broken windows, doing their best to keep the enemy from storming the door and finishing them off.

We have to blow a wall.

Moving to the next home would buy them precious seconds. Or they could go through the wall in that house, to the next one, or the one after that.

We could slip away… or flank the enemy.

But there was no way they could set a breaching charge and stay clear of the blast.

In a flash, Axe knew what he had to do. He let his M4 dangle on its sling, took the axe out of its improvised sheath, and prepared to attack the rear wall of the home.

Which is when the target, huddling docilely in the corner, playing his role perfectly, decided to attack.

4

THE AXE

The Hotel Grand Lagoon
Key Largo, Florida

"If the idiot hadn't yelled as he came at me, he might have had a chance," Axe told an enraptured Haley. "My rifle was dangling; the axe was in my right hand. I wouldn't have been able to shoot him. Had he knocked me down, he might have turned the axe on me."

"One of the guys would have shot him or pulled him off," Haley said.

"True. But it was dark and chaotic. If he had been quiet, he could have gotten lucky."

"But he had to use a war cry?" Nalen asked. "Work up the courage?"

"I guess. Anyway, I found out real quick how sharp the axe was."

Many Years Earlier
The Middle East

The target yelled as he lunged from the corner.

Axe had no time to think. He had just raised the axe above his head, ready to deliver a hammer blow onto the back wall. He'd figured that a few chops would put a hole in the mud wall, weakening it enough that some well-placed kicks would open up a space for them to slip through.

Instead, Axe turned his body at the attacker. His arm came down not on the wall but on the target's skull.

The blade of the axe cleaved the man's head open, slicing clean through the bone of the forehead.

The man dropped, forcing Axe to pull on the axe to yank it free.

"Target is down," Axe announced, turning back to the wall and delivering the blow to it as he'd originally intended. The blade tore a huge chunk of old, hardened mud from the wall. A few more hits opened up a small hole into the next home.

"Copy," Duke said, joining Axe at the back wall.

More hacks, along with kicks from Duke, and they had a hole large enough to squeeze through.

"Move," Duke ordered the Team. Axe was already wiggling through the opening.

Less than thirty seconds had passed since the first shots were fired.

In the other home, four men were on their feet in the dark room. Axe could see them with his NVGs, but they had clearly just gotten up as the firing started. They didn't have their act together yet.

They must have known about the operation—or they just reacted as anyone would if someone chopped down the back wall of their home and stepped through. They attacked.

Axe had no time to go for his gun. Instead, the axe became an extension of himself.

By the time Duke got his bulkier frame through the opening, it was over.

Axe dropped the axe, coated from top to bottom in the blood of his enemies. He rubbed his hands on his pants, removing enough of the blood off that he could grip his rifle well, then used the back of his arm to clean gore off his face.

"Smoke out," Tiger called from the other home.

"Good to go?" Duke asked as Axe raised his M4. Behind them, Rain Man slipped through the opening, then Tiger a moment later.

"Good to go."

5

AXE

"We snuck out the back, split up, and flanked the enemy. They never saw us coming," Axe remembered.

"You took out a lot of bad guys that night," Nalen said.

"I'm sure it was Duke who later told everyone the story—he saw the fight as he wiggled his way through the opening in the wall. He started calling me Axe again during the exfil." He chuckled. "No one called me Ape Man ever again."

They sat in companionable silence for a few minutes. Axe remembered his first Team: Duke, Tiger, Rain Man, JT, and the others. A few were gone. Others were instructors, had moved up the ranks, or had left their SEAL careers behind.

He'd thought it earlier in the week when he'd told Haley the story of him swinging between two buildings, and he felt it stronger tonight.

When I have some downtime, I've got to look them up.

"We'll stick with 'Blondie' for now," Nalen announced as he stood and stretched. "But it is operationally problematic. And possibly sexist.

So prepare yourself for a new call sign," he said to Haley, who also stood.

"'Hotshot'? 'Hardcore'? 'Harpy'?" Axe muttered as he followed them toward the hotel, leaving the fire behind.

"If we're going with mythology, I'd suggest 'Hera' over 'Harpy,'" Nalen said.

"Or we could stick with Blondie. I don't consider it sexist. It's... descriptive," Haley said, pulling her long blond hair back into a ponytail.

"Good night, you two," Nalen said, turning down the walkway to his room with Senator Woodran. "See you for a run in the morning,"

"Good night, Hammer," Axe said, then turned to Haley. "And good night..." He paused theatrically.

"Blondie," she said with a slow, convincing nod.

"Good night, Blondie," Axe said with a smile. He turned and walked to his room.

I can't wait to get her a better call sign.

———

———

OPERATION MAD DOG

1

THE TEAM

The gathering in this story (and the next three) takes place immediately after the ending of *A Team of Four*. To avoid spoilers, don't read the next four stories until you've finished *A Team of Four.*

Alex "Axe" Southmark's Cabin

Rural Virginia

Former SEAL Doug McBellin—known by his call sign of "Mad Dog" —looked around the cabin and smiled to himself. It had been a better night than he thought it would be. He hated to admit it, but being a part of Axe and Haley's missions had been extraordinarily fun. Defending Las Vegas from the "zombies," as he had dubbed them. Chasing down the mad doctor behind the whole thing.

I could get used to being a full-time member of their team. It's not a SEAL Team, but it's close.

Even the last few weeks at Axe's cabin had been fun.

I haven't felt this way since being on active duty.

Tonight, the whole crew was there: two teams of three, plus Haley —the fourth member of each.

On his side of the room, Mad Dog sat next to Axe and Admiral Nalen. While Axe—with his dark hair revealing more gray strands every day—could be funny at times, he was more straitlaced; the perfect straight man for Mad Dog's antics and funny lines.

They may roll their eyes at my schtick, but it lightens the mood and brings people together.

And retired Admiral William "Hammer" Nalen, in his white T-shirt and jeans, who Mad Dog had known only by reputation a few months before, had proven himself solid. A great warrior—and leader.

On the couch, the three intelligence analysts from Haley's office— the Central Analysis Group—sat shoulder to shoulder. There had been tension when they first arrived for dinner; warriors and analysts hanging out together didn't always click. The trigger pullers often didn't appreciate the geeks' hard work. And the analysts didn't often grasp how dangerous the missions were for the operators.

Gregory, the division's boss, was an obviously brilliant man. His graying, longer-than-regulation hair made him cool in Mad Dog's eyes. The other two—Nancy and Dave—were clearly a couple but weren't out in the open about it.

Funny they try to hide it. If I can tell after a few hours, surely everyone else can, too.

And at the end, in a chair next to the fireplace, sat Haley.

She's beautiful, intelligent, and fierce. The perfect woman—for someone.

From the start, it had been clear that he was too old for her. So were Axe and all the other retired SEALs.

He'd reminded the men with him on the mission in Mexico: Haley was off-limits.

She's like the little sister I never had—If my baby sis was a kick-ass warrior.

As he'd listened to her quietly finish her story earlier in the night— the first one she'd told since becoming a part-time asset in addition to her full-time analyst duties—he respected her even more.

"And that's the story," she's said when she'd finished.

Silence had hung in the air of the dim cabin, lit only by the fading glow of the fire and a few small lamps in the living room.

Dave had looked stricken to hear what Haley had gone through. Nancy seemed both horrified and motherly, like she wanted nothing more than to grab Haley and give her a big, reassuring hug.

Gregory sat stoically, but Doug could tell it pained him to hear the nitty-gritty details.

That's guilt. He feels bad—he must have sent her into harm's way.

Haley's story would improve with time and repeated telling. As she'd told it tonight, it was too factual. More like a debrief than a tale. But it was a good start. The bones were there—danger, intrigue, suspense. Still, it lacked humor.

Improve the pacing, skip over some of the gory bits, and highlight the absurdity of combat.

And it needed a better ending.

That he could help with.

He cleared his throat and nodded respectfully at Haley, acknowledging her story and all she'd gone through. Then he said in all seriousness, "And that's why my momma always said, 'Always wear clean underwear in case you're in an accident.'"

For a few seconds, he thought he'd gone too far. But then Haley laughed and shook her head at him. The mood lightened as the others groaned at his horrible joke.

"Luckily," Haley said, "my mother told me that too. It came in handy that night—I was wearing clean underwear. And," she admitted, "I had the exact same thought while they were cutting my clothes off before surgery." Then she added, "I'm going to use that next time I tell the story, if it's all right with you, 'Freddie'?"

Freddie? Mad Dog thought. *How the hell did she know that was my old call sign?*

"Freddie," Axe repeated, chuckling.

"No, no, no. Absolutely not," Doug said. "It used to be Freddie, yes. My first Team didn't have much of an imagination. You guys call me Mad Dog."

"It was your call sign, not just your middle name?" Haley asked. "I just took a guess, knowing your middle name is Frederick."

He didn't want to get into the other call signs he'd had the first few months of his time as an active-duty SEAL. "Dougie Fred," which led to "DF." Originally it served as shorthand for "Dougie Fred," but some of the more experienced guys treated it as a way to remind the smart-ass of his place. He could tell by context when it meant his name or when it referenced a new guy who was "a dumb f—."

Doug glanced at Axe and raised his eyebrow, asking for permission from the boss of the house, and got a nod in return.

"Fine," Doug said with an exaggerated sigh. "I'll tell you how I got from Freddie to Mad Dog."

He took a long pull of his beer and prepared himself. The details of that night many years before were seared into his memory. Glancing around the room, he confirmed he had everyone's attention.

"So no shit, there I was," he began, in the way these types of stories always did. "I can't tell you where, but it was on a mountain, it was a dark night, and we were greatly outnumbered. We were in trouble."

Doug took a second, recalling the bite of the cold desert air, the starless sky, and the rocky ground.

2

THE MOUNTAINS

Many Years Earlier
Somewhere in the Middle East

It was a long hike even by Navy SEAL standards.

The enemy controlled the entire area of soaring mountains and picturesque valleys. The eight SEALs had been dropped off at the far end of a valley where there was little risk of being seen by the enemy, who protected the high value target—HVT—the United States had deemed essential to kill or capture.

After a few hours of careful, quiet hiking, Doug—"Freddie" at the time—and the rest of the men were at the base of the mountain range. According to intel, their target was being sheltered in a system of caves on the other side, facing the next valley over.

There were likely enemy lookouts along the trail, especially further up the mountain, keeping watch.

The men, silently moving in the darkness like ghosts in the night, started up the steep, well-worn trail, night vision goggles on, rifles up and at the ready.

They killed the first sentry an hour later. The man had been half asleep, sitting on a blanket next to a large boulder at a switchback in the trail, his head leaning against the rock. The SEAL on point—Cooper—had covered the guard's mouth and jabbed a knife into the man's stomach and up, puncturing the heart.

The guard had a two-way radio, a powerful modern walkie-talkie, but it was turned off.

Are they on a schedule, Mad Dog wondered, *turning their radios on at certain times—every fifteen or thirty minutes—to report in?*

Or was battery conservation paramount, with the sentries only required to turn their radio on when they had something important to report to home base?

In other words, how much time before the dead man's absence was noted?

Up front, Cooper slipped the radio into his cargo pants pocket and resumed the upward hike, moving faster now. Freddie brought up the rear, regretting his muscular body and barrel chest, wishing he had longer legs and that he had done much more cardio training lately.

Two more guards were killed—both much less alert than they should have been.

They were expecting to hear helicopters. No one thought we'd land so far away and make such a long hike.

Finally, sweating despite the cold, high-altitude air, legs burning, Freddie took a knee facing back down the mountain trail, covering the Team's rear. Cooper would be poking his head over the rocky summit to scope out possible sentries on the other side.

Moments later, they were all up, moving slower as they started down the other side of the mountain and toward the cave system where dozens of enemy fighters guarded the man the SEALs had to capture—preferably—or kill if necessary.

3

THE CABIN

Alex "Axe" Southmark's Cabin
Rural Virginia

Mad Dog paused for a pull of his beer.

Those were the days, he thought.

"Man, I hated mountains," Axe muttered. "No matter how much I trained, they still wrecked my legs. I don't know how the locals did it."

"They were used to it," Nalen said. "They grew up playing on those trails, running up and down the mountains all day. No wonder it was so hard to fight them."

"True," Axe agreed.

"So did you get the HVT?" Nancy asked Mad Dog.

"Oh, we got him," Doug chuckled. "Never fear, the SEALs are here!"

Nalen chuckled while Axe shook his head. Doug ignored them both. "We crept downhill, which of course made our legs ache in other areas, snuck into the huge cave opening, and found our guy off a room in the back of the main cave. They left a decent number of men behind to guard the cave, but we figured out a way around them."

"Why weren't there more sentries along the way?" Haley asked.

"Half of the main force was out on an attack of an outpost. Our intel—" Mad Dog caught himself before he finished calling them geeks. "Our intel people figured out when the attack was planned for. The brass did nothing to stop it except give a warning to the men at the outpost to very quietly, very subtly prepare to be hit but not to give away that they knew what was coming." He shrugged. "It worked. Great coordination by command. The outpost troops killed a bunch of bad guys, took no casualties themselves, and we were able to get at our guy without problems."

"So when did you get your new name?" Haley asked.

Mad Dog paused for another long sip of beer, remembering.

Nalen answered for him. "No plan survives first contact with the enemy."

"Amen."

4

THE CAVE

Many Years Earlier
Somewhere in the Middle East

The large main room of the cave was dark except for a single, low-burning candle near the wall. Doug took one delicate step at a time, carefully lowering each foot to the ground. Around him, the enemy slept on the sandy floor of the cave in a random layout, with only thin blankets underneath them to ward off the cold of the ground.

Ahead of him, two of his teammates knelt next to the rounded entrance to one of the cave's many smaller rooms. They faced his direction, their weapons trained on the enemy in case he messed up and woke the men in the room.

18... 19... 20... 21... That's still a lot of bad guys. More than expected.

From the snoring, other men slept in nooks and smaller rooms off the main one. The enemy fighters appeared to be younger guys, barely out of their teens, and a few older ones. Several were missing limbs, either from injuries they'd sustained fighting Americans or from stepping on landmines that lay buried from past conflicts in the war-torn country.

These are reliable guys who weren't selected to go on the long hike to assault our outpost—dangerous, but not the A-team. They're guarding the cave and the HVT.

If it was just the group in the main cave, they could have taken everyone out. Some well-placed shots—easy with the guards on the ground asleep—and a grenade or two, and bye-bye, bad guys.

But if they didn't get everyone right away, the resulting firefight in the cave could go either way.

As he approached his teammates, Doug breathed easier. Stalking through the maze of sleeping men was a surreal experience that put his training to the test.

We really are ghosts.

Doug took a knee at the opening, freeing up one of the other men to duck back and help. Behind him, in the smaller cave off the main room, Cooper and another man had likely already injected the sleeping high-value target with a potent drug to knock him out. It would be a pain to carry him—and as the new guy, Doug would be expected to lug him longest and farthest. But with the HVT drugged, he wouldn't make noise. They could be in and out before anyone realized they'd been there.

Absolutely essential given the number of bad guys in here. And stealth is always better than a firefight.

Two SEALs were outside the cave as security. The rest of the guys were guarding side branches of the cave.

A few minutes later, Doug sensed that it was time for exfil. There was movement behind him and he got a light tap on his shoulder. As the last man in, he'd be first out, leading the Team back through the gauntlet of enemy soldiers, up the trail, over the peak of the mountain, and down through the valley.

Time to move out—and prove I can take point just as well as Cooper or the other guys.

He knew he wouldn't be allowed in the position long. The dead-weight body of the knocked-out target would be handed off to him as soon as the trail conditions allowed. None of the more experienced guys wanted to carry an extra hundred fifty pounds up, or down, the steep mountain trail.

One of the sleeping enemy rolled over on his blanket, wiggled, then coughed.

He's awake.

Doug's finger took in the slack of the trigger, ready to put a round through the man's head if he sat up and looked around.

The hand that had tapped his shoulder a moment before came back and pressed down.

Hold.

The Team could likely kill the men in the cave... at least in this main room. But there were other sections, and other caves, in the area. How many men had gone on the primary mission to attack the American outpost? When would they return? And how many stayed behind?

Once the shooting starts, we lose our element of surprise.

The tango was too far away for a stealth kill by hand, and even the quietest attack would be heard, felt, or sensed by the sleeping men near him.

They'd hear the crack of his neck if I did it by hand or smell the blood if I used a knife.

The restless tango rolled again, returning to face the back of the cave—right where Doug knelt.

Does the candle offer enough light to see me if he opens his eyes?

Doug kept his gun aimed at the man while rehearsing the moves needed.

I take the shot. Then I start picking off the ones nearest us. One shot, one kill. Someone else will join me and we'll take the bad guys out.

Then they'd all move. Back up the trail, over the ridge, and down, running and gunning all the way. Doable but very risky.

After what felt like an eternity, the hand on his shoulder gently directed him backward, deeper into the darkness of the secondary room. No words were spoken. None were needed. It was time for Plan B.

5

THE PROBLEM

Many Years Earlier
Somewhere in the Middle East

Doug walked backward, the hand of one of his teammates on his shoulder, guiding him. His aim didn't waver from the head of the restless tango on the floor of the cave until he turned a corner and lost sight of the man.

The intel nerds were convinced the cave system had a secondary exit. During their extensive surveillance, tangos appeared in the far valley without walking the long trail up and over the summit ridgeline. There had to be a way out—and in—but the location hadn't been identified.

Cooper must have decided the stealth approach was best and was willing to put his trust in the intel.

The intelligence is hopefully not always wrong.

The two men outside the cave would have been radioed to exfil on their own and—hopefully—meet up with the rest of the Team in the next valley, once they found a way out.

As the last man in the column, Doug didn't know where they were going or how they would find the way. He didn't have to. He was the new guy, and his job was to watch their "six."

The walls of the cave grew closer together in the green glow of his night vision goggles. Given the complete darkness, Cooper had popped infrared chemical lights so they could see.

They walked farther back into the mountain along a faint trail. At major junctions, the train of SEALs would stop while men darted down side paths, searching for the most likely way out.

Several minutes later, shouting came from the cave entrance.

Guess someone woke up and found their guy gone.

Would the enemy rush outside the cave and search the trail?

Or look deeper into the cave system, correctly guessing the ghosts who had infiltrated their camp had slipped into the depths of the mountain?

I'd do both.

The Team moved faster now, less worried about stumbling upon another group of fighters or hiding their escape.

The noise from the enemy faded. It sounded like most—possibly all—had exited the cave and were looking for them on the trails.

They know we like our technology—I bet they're geared up and ready to shoot down the helicopter they think is coming to land on the ridgeline and pick us up.

He hoped the two SEALs outside had gotten enough of a head start to sneak away.

After several more minutes, Doug smelled fresh, clean air—different from the smell of the cave. A minute later, he came to a halt as the men at the front of the column stopped and started stripping off their gear.

Oh no.

Nearby, the walls of the cave closed in, leaving the narrowest gap from top to bottom. He couldn't tell how far it extended, but the movements of his Team made it clear: this was the hidden exit. In the glow of the IR chem light, he eyed it carefully, trying to find a way around what his gut was screaming at him.

I'm not going to fit through that.

6

THE SQUEEZE

One by one, the men of his Team stripped off their weapons, plate carriers with armor, extra magazines, and knives.

Cooper was wiry and still had some trouble slipping through.

The next man up was "Petey," a burly guy—like Doug, but a bit thinner. He took off his shirt and handed his gear through the narrow gap, his arm stretching to reach Cooper.

So it's about two or three feet of tightness, then it must open up.

He struggled through the opening, his back pressed against the rock, head turned to the side, stepping to the right as his chest scraped the rock in front and behind him.

Then he got stuck.

Nothing was said. No one laughed, swore, or joked. But the mood changed.

We're screwed.

One man stepped forward and pushed. Cooper must have pulled. Blood flowed from Petey's chest and back as his skin was scraped raw from being forced through the slot.

It's like he's going through an opening between two cheese graters.

But Doug did his job, watching their rear while wondering how in the hell he would fit.

My chest has to be at least a few inches bigger than Petey's.

It took a minute, but they eventually got the man through.

The blood on the rock, along with the thinner builds of the next several men, made it relatively easy for them to get out.

Finally, it was Doug's turn. He quickly stripped off his gear and clothes, all the way down to his underwear. He took his pistol from the holster and held it in his left hand, just in case. Then he used the hydration bladder from his pack to douse himself with water.

It might make me just slippery enough to get through.

Finally, he passed all the gear across—except the pistol—stretching in an attempt to reach his teammate on the far side.

Doug turned sideways and started wiggling. He only got a few inches before his barrel chest stopped him.

This is going to hurt.

Exhaling, he shrunk as small as he could and kept moving.

Tiny rocks tore into his skin, scraping it raw at first, then cutting deeper as the gap narrowed more.

Blood flowed and the pain came.

Adapt and overcome.

He couldn't draw in a full breath—he'd get permanently stuck. So he took tiny breaths and fought to control his mind.

I'm fine. I do not have to breathe deeply.

He thought of BUD/S, the SEAL training program designed to weed out the weak, the uncommitted, the candidates who couldn't keep going when the going got tough—or when things turned awful, horrible, and painful.

Doug stretched out his right arm, but he wasn't far enough along to grasp the hand of the SEAL on the far side, though he could feel the movement of air from the man reaching.

His back and chest were on fire from the pain but the blood, now flowing freely, made him just slippery enough for him to keep moving, inch by inch.

Footsteps came from up the tunnel.

Shit. They sent people back here to find us or ambush us coming down the other side of the mountain.

It didn't matter which. In a moment, he would be discovered wedged into the narrow gap.

Doug raised his arm with the pistol but couldn't get a good angle. And wiggling around had stopped his momentum.

He was stuck and would only be able to shoot someone right next to him—if they didn't kill him first.

7

THE MAD DOG

Many Years Earlier
Somewhere in the Middle East

Doug released every last bit of air from his lungs, fighting to compress his chest to its smallest possible size. Then he wrenched himself another inch through the cheese graters, ignoring the pain.

If they see me, I'm dead.

His mind considered his limited options.

The gap narrowed above his head, leaving no room for his teammates to fire over the top of him at the men coming down the tunnel.

He was moving as fast as he could, fighting for each inch of progress. Cooper—the thinnest of the Team and likely the man on the other side reaching for his hand—couldn't grab him yet to help.

If I can make it a bit farther, he'll be able to pull.

Still looking back into the tunnel, without his NVGs, which he'd taken off and passed along, Doug saw a faint, flickering glow.

Thank God. They've got a damn candle and can't run fast without it blowing out.

Without much debate, he went with the crazy idea that popped into his mind. The Navy had introduced working dogs to the fight, bringing them along on raids where the animals would come in handy sniffing out explosives or finding bad guys trying to hide.

The enemy hated the dogs and were rightly terrified of them. The powerful, well-trained animals had a reputation of being dangerous and deadly to anyone who hid, ran, or fought.

A man—even a warrior like the SEALs—could be reasoned with.

The dogs? Not so much.

The warrior dogs were usually silent but would bark, growl, or snarl on command. The threatening noises often worked so well, the warriors didn't have to risk their dogs' lives sending them into a building or other area. Often, the enemy would come out from hiding or surrender just from hearing the dangerous sounds from the dogs.

Doug growled, imitating one of the attack dogs. The low rumble lasted only a second before his breath gave out.

Was it enough?

The footsteps faltered.

The flickering glow stopped moving.

They're buying it.

He guessed the enemy knew they had found the intruders but were reluctant to face off against a fierce Navy SEAL dog.

He growled louder, sounding convincing to his own ears—and hopefully to the tangos in the tunnel.

Wiggling a bit more while continuing to growl as much as his tiny gasps of air allowed, he flailed with his right arm.

His fingertips grazed Cooper's hand.

Come on, another inch.

He forced himself further along, leaving more skin, chest hair, and blood behind.

The candlelight moved as the tangos crept closer.

Doug snarled like a mad dog, his teeth bared, selling the ruse with every ounce of his soul.

The light stopped.

Cooper's hand locked onto his hand and pulled.

Doug kept snarling, then switched to barking as the men shuffled bravely closer, still out of sight around a bend in the tunnel.

A second later, he popped free, falling on top of Cooper.

Blind in the darkness without his NVGs, he got himself up and was hustled away from the gap.

THE GOOD OLD DAYS

Alex "Axe" Southmark's Cabin
Rural Virginia

For a few seconds, Mad Dog was lost in the memory of the cave.

Then Axe spoke. "Good times," he said, raising his beer.

"Good times," Mad Dog repeated, along with Nalen and the others, then took a drink.

"We didn't talk much on the hike out," Mad Dog said, finishing up the story. "We'd avoided the worst of the mountain hiking with our shortcut. And they only made me carry the drugged HVT for a few miles. I didn't mind much—I had him in a firefighter's carry across my shoulder. It only hurt when he scraped my back or chest—and it showed the senior guys I could handle myself."

"Did the guys in the tunnel come after you?" Nancy asked.

"Well, they tried…" He mimed an explosion. "Boom! Cooper must have accidentally left a few grenades attached to trip wires in the gap."

"Accidents happen all the time," Axe said with a nod.

"Sure do. Anyway, by the time we got back to base, I was no longer 'Freddie.' I was 'Mad Dog.' Have been ever since."

"It suited you even before I heard the story," Haley told him. "I can't picture you as anything else."

And it's so much better than "DF."

Mad Dog waited. The story wasn't quite finished.

Haley caught on. "What aren't you telling us? Did you grab the wrong guy? 'The intelligence is always wrong'?"

He shook his head. "Nope. The intel was right on. No, see, I wasn't the only guy who got a new nickname that night."

Admiral Nalen chuckled. "I think I know. Or at least what I would call him. It's Petey, right?"

Mad Dog nodded. "Yep. Poor Petey had gotten stuck first, so despite not having an ounce of fat on him, from that night on he was 'Piggy.'"

He hated that name at first but grew to like it.

"To Piggy—and all the other warriors who led the way," Axe said.

Once more, they all toasted.

Mad Dog relaxed, a contented smile on his face, and waited for one of the others to tell a tale.

OPERATION PAST DUE

1

THE MOON

Alex "Axe" Southmark's Cabin
Rural Virginia

Axe relaxed fully for the first time in weeks. In his home, surrounded by other warriors—and Haley's intelligence team from the Central Analysis Group office—he felt at peace.

Once again, the fire had died down, leaving only embers in the fireplace. The night was still young, but Gregory, Nancy, and Dave had a long ride back to their homes in the DC area. They would have to get going soon.

"Speaking of risky missions," Mad Dog said. He'd told a funny story about earning his call sign but was apparently not done for the night. "I heard a rumor once and have always wondered if it was true," Mad Dog said, looking at Axe as he tried to hold back a grin.

What is this maniac talking about? Axe wondered.

Haley had finally told her own hair-raising story filled with tension and drama. Axe didn't want to upstage her. And Mad Dog's tale had been both exciting and funny.

But traditionally, a gathering like tonight called for several stories to be told. Recounting past missions reinforced lessons learned. Many of their missions were Top Secret; reports were written, but they wouldn't contain the nitty-gritty details. The men on the ground, in the thick of the action, needed to tell their sides of the stories. They would laugh—and occasionally cry—while reliving the adventures, horrors, or sheer chaos of both successful and less-than-perfect operations.

"You'll have to correct me if I have my details wrong," Mad Dog continued, "but it was a jungle mission to take out a terrorist..." His eyes gleamed in the fading glow of the fireplace.

Oh, hell. Do I really want to tell that story?

"Not much of a tale," Axe explained, downplaying the operation. "We went in, got the job done, and got out."

He didn't want to admit how terrified he'd been—or how close he'd come to leaving this world in pieces.

Nancy and Dave leaned forward expectantly. They wanted to hear more.

Nalen chuckled and took a sip of his beer.

I bet he's heard this one—or at least read the report.

"What aren't you telling us?" Haley asked. "Knowing Mad Dog, there's something more to the story."

Mad Dog shrugged, giving her a "Who, me?" look.

It had been many years since that night, but it was stuck in Axe's memory as if it had been last week. *Why not? It might be good for everyone to hear how far SEALs will go to complete a mission.*

"Um, was there really a...?" Mad Dog stopped, hinting at the ending without giving it away to the rest of the group.

Axe ignored him.

Remembering that night, Axe began in the traditional way. "So no shit, there I was. I can't tell you where, of course, but it was a hot night in a swamp. The water was black and stank, and the moon was coming up. It was a horrible time for an assault." He shrugged. "But sometimes it is what it is."

"It is what it is," Mad Dog and Nalen muttered under their breath and raised their beers in a toast.

And with that, Axe was back on a small, flat-bottom boat in the middle of the swamp.

2

EMBRACE THE SUCK

Many Years Earlier
Somewhere in South Asia

Axe listened as Duke, their team lead, wrapped up the briefing. Everyone was unhappy with the plan.

"Yes, the conditions are less than ideal," Duke summed up. "The moonlight will be an issue. The swamp is unfamiliar territory. And the timing is tight. But at least there are snakes," he joked.

The dark humor lightened the mood.

"We can do this. And it has to be done now. This is the one night the target will be accessible. He's past due to be taken out. If the intel is wrong and he's not there, or we can't get to him, so be it. But we have to try."

The ramifications if we fail are bad.

Tonight, they weren't risking only their lives. Failure meant the enemy encampment would have to be destroyed by the air, with missiles fired from either a jet or a helicopter. To all the SEALs in the room, and the brass, this was unacceptable. It meant the deaths of women who had been abducted from a nearby village to cook and clean for the terrorists in the camp.

"So let's get in, shoot this asshole in the head, and get out," Duke finished up.

The terrorist leader ruled with an iron fist. The intelligence nerds were convinced that killing him would either dissolve his small band of men or cause enough in-fighting to make it ineffective. The women would likely be released as the leader's followers left the dismal swamp and returned to their homes—where they would be killed or captured in due time.

Axe, Duke, JT—the Team's best sniper—and Rain Man were on the main assault team. Others were to be ready at the edge of the swamp as a quick reaction force, though "quick" and navigating the swamp were mutually exclusive.

More men would be waiting in a helicopter at a staging area nearby. They would be on hand to attempt to fast-rope through the thick canopy of the swamp if absolutely necessary. Getting down looked impossible, but they would try if the others were in danger.

While gearing up, the men allowed themselves five minutes to complain. They would get it all out of their system, leaving behind any negativity so they could fully focus on the mission. Despite their concerns, their tone was more matter-of-fact than truly upset. They had a job to do, they were the best chance the innocent women in the camp had, and they were all fine with risking their lives to take out an evil man and save his captives. Still…

"The 'quick' reaction force is a joke," Rain Man said.

"Yep," Duke nodded. Even though he was in charge, he was right there with them.

"We have no idea what we'll find there," JT said. They didn't have much intel to go on due to the difficulty of penetrating the overhead cover. "The tango might not be there. Or he could be hiding in a hut with trees preventing a clean shot."

"True," Duke said.

"And the snakes," Axe muttered. He didn't mind the sharks or stingrays in the ocean, but the jungle wasn't his favorite place. And swamps were worse. Too many creepy-crawly things for his comfort.

His words made the others pause for a moment before finishing their gear check.

"Are we done?" Duke asked.

There were nods all around.

"Then let's go embrace the suck."

3

THE SWAMP

Alex "Axe" Southmark's Cabin
Rural Virginia

"Embrace the suck," Nalen and Mad Dog muttered together, repeating the famous SEAL mantra. It meant not only doing what needed to be done, despite the difficulties or how uncomfortable it was, but embracing how bad it was; changing the mindset made the job easier.

"Been there, done that," Mad Dog said.

"Embrace it we did," Axe said with a chuckle. "It was bad. I much prefer the ocean or the desert to the swamp."

"Was the tango there?" Haley asked. "Or was the intelligence wrong?"

She's beating me to it.

"No, the intelligence wasn't wrong this time. But first, we had to get there."

Many Years Earlier
Somewhere in South Asia

The moon was up. There was plenty of light to see by. Night vision goggles weren't needed. It was the worst possible evening for a stealth approach, but at least they had help.

The Navy Special Warfare Combat Craft Crewman, the special boat team member who piloted their flat-bottom boat, said they could go anywhere—the boat draft was only ten inches. They had a quiet motor to travel upriver, and Kyle—the crewman—had a pole to use once they got into the peat swamp forest.

The mission went fine until they tried to leave the river and enter the swamp to approach the terrorists' camp.

They only got ten feet before they stopped. The swamp here looked like a typical jungle—if the jungle had flooded. Small- and medium-sized trees grew close together, completely blocking their path.

Kyle poled the boat backward, away from the dead end and onto the main stretch of river.

He moved the boat upstream to another spot previously identified by satellite as being a likely ingress point. They got two boat lengths before the foliage blocked their path.

Two other approaches turned them back.

They faced a choice.

They could use the main path to the camp, keeping a close eye out for guards and eliminating them one by one as they drew closer to their target. They'd be able to stay in the boat and cover the distance quickly, easily, and safely—unless they didn't notice a sentry in time, or missed one who let them pass only to radio his comrades to set up a full ambush further along the narrower river. Then they'd be under fire and in trouble.

Or they could swim, ditching the boat, and use the same obvious, predictable path.

Now that they saw the swamp firsthand, the other option—bushwhacking a direct path to the terrorists' hideout—was out.

Duke stripped off his non-essential gear, and the others followed suit. Face masks, snorkels, and fins were pulled out of their gear bags and slipped on. Rifles were slung across their backs.

They slipped into the warm water silently and nodded to Kyle, who would wait for them.

They swam upstream.

Once they left the main river, turning into the stream to the encampment, the water became more stagnant.

Axe spotted the first sentry. A man sat smoking in a wooden boat, half paying attention.

They easily submerged and passed him by, electing to leave him alive in case there were frequent radio checks. These men weren't stupid, though their trust in the swamp to protect them was misplaced.

Or they didn't think anyone would be crazy enough to swim upstream to their camp.

Axe was glad America's enemies continued to underestimate the SEALs.

The water path narrowed more and more, from over one hundred feet wide to fifty, then thirty, and finally only ten.

They were close.

They passed two more sentries on the approach. One was wide awake and alert. The other was sleeping, snoring so loudly they knew exactly where he was long before they reached the bend in the pathway where he lay in a small wooden boat tied to a submerged tree.

Axe led the way, moving slowly and silently through the water, skirting the edge of the trees in the narrow waterway.

The camp came into view after another bend in the river. It was on land, rising a few feet from the dark water. Dozens of logs had been sunken into the ground to form pylons. Wide boards and other scrap lumber had been laid out in a semi-professional manner to form a vast deck five feet off the ground.

The wooden base covered the small island, which was about the size of two basketball courts side by side. The camp consisted of four large white tents that were tall enough to stand up in and several smaller tents along the perimeter.

A flat-bottom boat, similar to the skiff they had used to get up the river, was tied to a pylon next to a crude wooden ladder. It had a powerful outboard engine.

Axe stopped in the shadows of the trees, nearly lying flat on the mucky bottom to remain underwater. He glanced back at JT, who shook his head.

He has no shot.

There were trees, but they would be impossible to climb without making noise. So they would have to do this the old-fashioned way: sneak in and kill the target—hopefully without stirring up a hornet's nest of terrorists and starting a deadly, up-close-and-personal firefight.

After a minute of careful observation, Axe saw the sentry on duty —head to his chest, asleep... or at least "resting his eyes." An AK lay across the man's lap.

Of course. Why stay awake in the middle of the swamp, on the far side of three of your buddies who are guarding the approach?

Axe checked in with Duke, who had seen the guard and would now lead the way.

Guard first, then the rest.

They switched the order, with Duke slowly swimming across the narrow gap between the trees and the platform, followed by Rain Man and then JT, who was just as good at hand-to-hand combat as he was in his role as a sniper.

Axe covered the approach of the other three. He would shoot the guard with his suppressed M4 should he awaken and catch a glimpse of the attackers. It wouldn't be ideal, but the swamp was noisy enough with the local fauna that the shot might go unnoticed. And it sure beat the alternative of the sentry yelling out a warning while opening fire on the SEALs.

Duke climbed the ladder, followed close behind by Rain Man. Before JT was halfway up, Duke had already slit the throat of the guard and left him sitting in his chair.

It was time for Axe to cross the water.

As soon as he started swimming, he had a feeling.

I'm not alone.

Had they missed a guard? Would the terrorists really make a man sit on a boat near the island in addition to the sentry at the edge of the platform?

He swam quicker, his feeling changing from unease to concern.

There was a *swish* sound from the shallow water ten feet up the bank.

Another noise made his blood run cold: a tiny *glup*.

That's the sound of water closing over the top of something submerging.

Something very large had slipped into the water behind him.

4

GOOD TIMES

Alex "Axe" Southmark's Cabin
Rural Virginia

"Wait! The suspense is killing me," Mad Dog said, entirely serious. "Before you continue, I have to know—did you make it?"

Axe knew the question had been coming, but he still had to laugh at the crazy man's antics. Mad Dog had been relatively quiet and calm the last few weeks they'd spent together, but tonight he had an audience and was playing to them.

"You'll just have to hear the rest of the story. I can tell you this, though: I've never swum so fast in my life as I did right then."

Many Years Earlier
Somewhere in South Asia

Axe suspected he didn't have a chance, but he still had to try. The crocodile—he knew in his gut that's what he was up against—was in its natural element. Its speed in the water easily outmatched his.

But not its motivation.

I bet I want to live more than it wants to eat me.

Plus, Axe had a head start.

If we hadn't stopped where we did, I'd be dead right now.

As he kicked frantically with his fins and pulled with his arms, his M4 slung once again across his back, Axe had to balance speed with moving quietly. But after a second, he stopped worrying about potentially being heard by the terrorists in the camp and focused on the immediate danger of a huge prehistoric beast ending his Navy SEAL career much too early.

This is not how I want to go out!

Axe made it to the ladder, his senses screaming at him. Danger was very close. He was about to die.

Alex "Axe" Southmark's Cabin
Rural Virginia

Axe paused and made eye contact, first with Admiral Nalen, then Mad Dog, and finally Haley.

"You know that feeling," he said.

He didn't have to ask. Each of the warriors in the room had faced death. The story Haley had finished earlier touched on it.

Axe had felt the hand of God—or grace, providence, luck, whatever.

There had also been several times Death had reached for him. Axe had slipped through his fingers… so far.

Nalen, Mad Dog, and Haley nodded silently and sipped their beers.

Mine won't be the last story told tonight.

They didn't usually talk about the truly close calls. There often wasn't much humor in those stories. But tonight, the memories would be unwrapped and the tales told. It would be healing for the SEALs, though Axe had to wonder how it would affect the non-warriors in the group.

He took a sip of his beer, remembering the night in the swamp.

"Well?" Nancy said. "Don't leave us hanging!"

He chuckled and nodded. "So no shit, there I was, on the ladder…"

Many Years Earlier
Somewhere in South Asia

Axe never considered stopping to take off his fins. He lunged for the lowest rung on the ladder and hauled himself up, certain the beast was within inches of snapping down on his legs and dragging him underwater.

The fins slapped uselessly on the ladder, so he used only his arms to pull himself up higher as quickly as he could. The line holding the boat to the pylon nearly got wrapped around his arm, but he avoided it at the last moment.

He'd only been on the ladder a few seconds when he instinctively did a pull-up on the ladder rung and brought his knees to his chest, tucking into a ball.

A dark mass leaped out of the water. The crocodile's powerful jaws snapped closed on the air where Axe's legs had been an instant earlier.

Then the enormous beast crashed back into the water, breaking the line to the boat as he fell on it.

Alex "Axe" Southmark's Cabin
Rural Virginia

"To make a long story short," Axe said, "the terrorists came to investigate the commotion. We took them out. Accomplished our mission. Saved the abducted women—and a few men taken for the heavier chores."

Axe wondered if any of them would put it together.

It was Nancy, the sharp senior intelligence analyst, who caught it. "The boat was your way back."

Nailed it.

It took another few seconds, but first Mad Dog smiled appreciatively. Then it dawned on Nalen. Finally, Haley got it. But Gregory, Nancy, and Dave hadn't figured the rest out.

"Swimming back," Axe continued slowly, "especially with the people taken hostage, was out. Plus, there were still the sentries on the way back to take care of. We needed the boat that had drifted away. The croc was still out there and obviously hungry, so…" He trailed off with a shrug.

"No!" Nancy said, catching on.

"Smart," Gregory said with approval.

"We tossed the dead terrorists off the back of the island platform," Axe said. "Within minutes, there was a feeding frenzy. We think it was only one male—they're territorial—but several females came to our little midnight buffet in the swamp. We saw the one who had come after me. I swear he was three times my length, nose to tail. Eighteen feet, easy."

"And when they were feeding on the far end…" Dave said.

Axe nodded. "Yep. I'm the one who got chased by the crocodile, which caused the line to break, so I got to swim after the boat."

"Good times," Nalen muttered.

"Good times," Axe, Mad Dog, and Haley said quietly, repeating the mantra.

"But no gator wrestling?" Mad Dog asked.

"Sorry, brother. None."

Mad Dog faked dejection. "Bummer. But I guess you made it, and I'm glad for that."

"Thanks. Me too."

There was quiet for a moment while they all digested the story.

"Speaking of the hand of Death," Mad Dog started.

His face looked haunted, not at all like the smart-ass he could often be.

He took a big sip of his beer, burped quietly, and leaned forward in his chair. "So no shit, there I was…" Mad Dog said.

———————

———————

OPERATION HAMMER TIME

1

ANCIENT HISTORY

Alex "Axe" Southmark's Cabin
Rural Virginia

As usual at these nights of storytelling and camaraderie, Admiral William "Hammer" Nalen kept quiet, content to sip a beer and listen to the younger guys—and Haley—tell their stories.

Tonight, after yet another mission in which he had helped save the world, was no different.

Mad Dog, who had earlier told his funny cheese grater story, turned to look at him sitting near the kitchen—close enough to the rest of the group to be a part of it yet far enough away to subtly make a point: he was the old guy.

The audience, not a teller of tales.

Mad Dog's face had lost all trace of the animation it had shown earlier as he spoke of—and acted out—fitting his body through the tight squeeze in the tunnel where he'd earned his call sign.

"I'd love to hear about your time on the Teams, Admiral," Mad Dog said quietly.

William couldn't decide whether the man was serious or messing with him. He sounded respectful, but...

Doug—"Mad Dog"—was an incredible warrior. Rock-solid reliable. And by throwing out his corny humor at exactly the right moment, he helped make even the worst situations bearable.

But the routine could also get old quickly.

Axe cleared his throat from nearby. "I think we would all enjoy the history lesson, Hammer, if you're up for it. No pressure, though."

William sipped his beer, debating.

Why not? With a caveat, though.

"What you have to realize from the start is that it was another time," he began.

"That makes sense," Mad Dog said, having a hard time keeping a grin off his face. "Probably hard to fight wars with dinosaurs roaming around."

What a pain in the ass. But damn, it feels good to be one of the guys again.

"Yes, the dinosaurs were often a problem," William said. "Especially the velociraptors. SEALs these days wouldn't stand a chance. They don't make 'em like they used to."

The mood, heavy after Haley's story about how the previous mission ended, had lightened during Mad Dog's tale of scraping off his manly chest hair in the cave and Axe's story of the jungle.

Now it lightened further.

"Seriously, though," William said, his voice quiet. "When I was first in the Teams, we weren't in the middle of wars in the Middle East yet."

"Or 'conflicts,' as the politicians call them," Mad Dog muttered.

"Much of my time—before I moved up the ranks and out of the field—involved close protection details overseas, some drug dealer interdiction, and tons of training. We prepped for wars that never arrived. Well," he added, "not until after I gained rank."

He leaned forward, making his point. "The problem with most of my stories from that time is they aren't the crazy, 'you-can't-make-this-shit-up' tales told while drinking beers with buds. Most of them involve sending men into harm's way."

He looked at each of the people in the room, starting with the operators—Mad Dog and Axe. They met his gaze evenly. They'd long ago come to terms with the possibility of not coming back from a mission.

William moved on to the analysts—Gregory, Nancy, and Dave, sitting relaxed on the couch after the night's dinner with the warriors had gone well. They understood in an abstract way how their intel and analysis were used, but they likely couldn't truly grasp what it felt like to go out into the world for an operation and not know whether you'd live through the night.

Next: Haley, who knew all too well the danger.

And last, Mariana—the potential newest member of the team—who only had an inkling of what she might be getting into.

William had effectively killed the fun mood Mad Dog had achieved.

"Now, I could tell you about the op where I earned my call sign," William said with a smile, making an effort to recapture the banter from earlier. "Or about the time we rode into combat on the backs of a herd of stegosaurs."

"Ouch," Haley said. The others looked her way.

No one else knows what they look like.

"What?" Haley said. "I loved dinosaurs as a kid. Stegosaurus is the tank-like dinosaur with the fan-blade plates sticking up from their backs."

"Oh, I want to hear more about them!" Mad Dog said.

"But instead," William continued, ignoring the short, barrel-chested man, "I'll tell you a short story about cologne."

"Oh, I love Germany," Nancy said.

William kept the smile off his face. She'd figure it out as he told the story.

He took a sip of his beer and thought about the mission where he and his men had learned a valuable lesson. Then he began in the traditional way. "So no shit, there I was…"

2

THE HUNT

Many Years Earlier
Somewhere in Latin America

Most of the men were green—they'd never been in combat.

They'd spent years training for every imaginable scenario. From skydiving into a secure compound to spending hours underwater setting demolition charges, they were experienced in every way—except in real-world, life-and-death action.

Of the eight men on this portion of the operation, six had never fired a shot on an actual mission, or come remotely close to killing.

In the QRF—quick reaction force—that would surround the target location to guard against escapees, it was the same: two senior, experienced men with six other highly trained but untested SEALs.

But all sixteen were ready, willing, and able to get the job done.

William surveyed the area through his night vision goggles, breathing slowly and doing everything in his power to convince his mind that tonight was exactly the same as any of the countless training missions they'd all been on.

Just another day at the office.

He was the third man in the stack, directly in front of their team lead, who was one of the mission's experienced men.

They crept along an alleyway behind expensive homes—or at least, expensive for this second-world country. They didn't compare to the drug lords' mansions in Mexico, but to the standards of this area, they were opulent: white, two-story houses on sprawling compounds, surrounded by tall fences topped with glass shards or rolls of razor wire. They were a few miles outside the city center but close enough to the restaurants, bars, and nightclubs that made the area famous and popular.

William and the other men moved down the narrow alley between whitewashed stone walls with solid wooden gates set on thick hinges. It wouldn't be difficult to blow up a gate and get inside quickly, but that would give away the element of surprise tonight's operation called for.

William sensed they were stopping before the fists of the men in front of him went up. He raised his own fist to signal the men trailing him.

So far, so good.

The night was dark. He was confident they hadn't been seen. And they had reached the objective without the ever-present local dogs barking, which was one of the concerns during the mission brief.

William quickly shrugged off his pack and removed the telescoping ladder, which he extended, hating the soft noise it made in the quiet night.

No one can hear that except us.

He stood up the ladder and let its padded ends gently kiss the wall, making no noise.

The SEAL who had been in front of him climbed the ladder in a flash while William held it firm, keeping it still and quiet.

Be careful up there.

There were at least two guards patrolling the backyard, according to the intel. The man atop the ladder would hopefully be able to see both in his night vision goggles. With any luck, he'd use his suppressed rifle to eliminate them, jump to the ground on the far side, and unlock the gate so the rest of the Team could join him in the assault of the home.

With any luck.

3

MEMORIES

Alex "Axe" Southmark's Cabin
Rural Virginia

William paused for a sip of his beer. It felt strange to talk of a long-ago mission. But at the same time, it felt good.

It's been too long since I told stories.

The men and women in the room hung on his every word, no doubt picturing themselves on the mission. The warriors would be considering how they would handle the operation's challenges. Or recalling being in similar situations in other foreign countries.

"Let me guess," Haley asked, trying to make light of the Teams' common saying, though it likely hit too close to home for her, Nancy, and Dave. "The intel is always wrong?"

"No," William answered. "They were right this time."

"But," Mad Dog said with a big grin, "instead of two guards, there were two T-Rex?"

"Nope. Two guards. Two shots."

"That's it?" Mad Dog asked. "Didn't they teach you guys how to tell stories back then?"

William had to laugh. "I told you, my stories don't involve as much wild action as yours do." He leaned forward, acting serious. "Probably because back then we didn't do stupid shit and get ourselves stuck in caves."

Mad Dog chuckled. "That's probably it. Please, continue."

"So we got into the backyard of this mini compound in the city with no one the wiser."

Many Years Earlier
Somewhere in Latin America

William was the locksmith of the group. He'd spent hour after patient hour learning how to pick every type of lock, keeping up with the skill and feel by practicing daily during deployment.

He unlocked the doorknob and deadbolt, though it took longer than he wanted. The pressure of having guards inside ready to kill them if he made too much noise, plus seven of his guys relying on him to get the job done, slowed him down. It was a lot different from picking practice locks back at base.

Inside, all the remaining guards were easily handled. They were no match for the SEALs with their day-in, day-out training.

But after that, the mission went to hell.

Their target wasn't home.

Their intel source—the SEALs hadn't been told who it was or how they came about the information—claimed their target would definitely be in the house that night. The playboy drug dealer often spent nights —sometimes several in a row—at nightclubs or in the homes of ladies he met. But the source guaranteed he would be in the house.

What changed?

William had a horrible thought.

What if we have the wrong night?

Or the intel was wrong.

The intel is always wrong.

All this risk for nothing?

And with the dead guards littering the house and grounds, the target would know he was in danger and disappear.

Damn it!

They searched the house from bottom to top.

Nothing.

They did it again, slower, more methodically despite being extremely thorough the first time.

Still nothing.

There were no safe rooms or hidden areas.

The drug dealer hadn't escaped out the front or sides—the QRF men had eyes on every exit from the house.

Two of the SEALs opened a second-floor window and climbed out, confirming the roof was empty.

The target had vanished.

The first real-life, non-training mission most of the men had been on was a complete failure.

4

THE COLOGNE

Alex "Axe" Southmark's Cabin
Rural Virginia

The analysts and warriors sat still as William paused for a much-needed sip of beer. He stared at the fire but was back in that dark house with its air conditioner blasting in an effort to keep out the hot, humid night air of the city.

"That's it?" Mad Dog asked after a long silence. "Your first mission was a dud?"

"I knew it," Haley said, only half-joking. "The intel is always wrong. Or it was until Nancy, Dave, and I got on the scene, right?"

William smiled. "You have all been great. Without your intel..." He trailed off. Everyone in the room knew that without Haley's uncanny intuition, along with Gregory's leadership and Nancy and Dave's analytical minds, the country would have been in trouble several times over.

"No. The intel was right, as I said. We just had to find the damn guy."

"Ah!" Nancy said with a look of realization. "I get it."

William smiled at her and nodded. "It was pretty tense there for a while…"

Many Years Earlier
Somewhere in Latin America

"Where the hell is he?" their team lead asked with steel in his voice. "He's supposed to be here. Find him."

William grabbed his buddy, a great warrior with the call sign of "Toad," who would die later that year in a stupid training accident, and followed a hunch. He led Toad to the huge main bathroom.

They again found nothing.

William and Toad moved to the adjacent primary bedroom and stood at the foot of the bed, looking around in their NVGs at the five-piece bedroom set: dresser, two nightstands, mirror, and platform bed.

"Did anyone check under the bed?" William asked Toad. Clutching their weapons, they lowered down and looked.

Nothing. Of course someone checked under the bed.

"Close the damn window," William told Toad. The two SEALs who inspected the roof had left it slightly open.

Shit. Could he have hidden somewhere while we searched the room and cleared the roof, then slipped out the window afterward?

"Check the roof," he said with a grin. Toad had worked his ass off to overcome a fear of heights. The instructors at BUD/S had "helped," as had his teammates once assigned to a squad. At every opportunity involving cliffs, roofs, or other high, exposed situations, the message was the same. "Toad, come on up."

"Asshole," Toad muttered as he removed the screen.

William suspected the target hadn't slipped out. Or if he had, he was a cool operator to be on the run, climb out the window, and hang around long enough to jam the screen back into place before continuing his escape.

All without the SEALs outside seeing him.

He still let Toad wiggle out, carefully stand on the window ledge, and stretch up to inspect the roof.

"Nothing here."

"You think we should climb all the way up, go over the top, and check the other side?"

"Screw you," Toad said. He finally figured out William was messing with him. "The guys outside can see there's no one on the roof."

William helped Toad back inside. They fitted the screen back on—it may have been a drug lord's house, but they could still be considerate—and it would serve as a warning signal if they heard anyone taking it out.

Toad slammed the window shut and looked around the room. "Where the hell is he?"

The bureau drawers had been pulled out to confirm they were real and not a hiding place, and pulled away from the wall to make sure there were no hidden compartments behind it.

The nightstands were too small for a person, but the SEALs who had previously searched the room had taken those drawers out, too, and also pulled them away from the wall.

The mirror?

With a gesture of his head, he got Toad to aim his weapon at the mirror. Then William lifted it from the wall, revealing…

Nothing but the wall.

Damn it.

Something still bothered William about the room. Or the bathroom. Somewhere nearby. He closed his eyes and stilled his mind.

After a few breaths, he had it.

He smelled cologne.

Moving closer to the bathroom, he breathed in.

Yes. Naturally. This is where he douses himself with it every morning. Or night. Whenever.

He moved back to his spot near the mirror he'd left leaning against the wall. He repeated the process, closing his eyes again and breathing in.

The scent wasn't as strong, but it was there. And not wafting in from the bathroom, either.

The sheets?

The king bed's sheets were jumbled like they'd been slept in recently. But they were much too flat to hide a person.

Still, William moved closer, following his nose.

He glanced at Toad, who had gone quiet and still, sensing his partner was onto something.

Here.

The smell of expensive men's cologne was stronger here. He picked up the sheets. They smelled of laundry detergent.

The bed?

He looked at Toad and shrugged. The bed consisted of a mattress on a platform, an inch-thick piece of dark wood... or at least, it looked dark in the green glow of the night vision goggles.

William bent low again, looking under the bed. He could smell the cologne better.

A trap door?

He considered the layout of the house. Below the bedroom was a dining room. There wouldn't be enough space for a trapdoor or a hiding place. And the smell was strongest right here, not beneath the bed.

When all the other options are eliminated...

Their team lead's voice came through the radio. "This is a bust. We're moving out. Assemble at the back door in one." It was time to leave.

William wasn't new to the Team. He'd been active for a while, though he was still considered a noob by the team lead and the other guys who had real combat experience. But the SEAL training kicked in. He clicked his mic once, signaling a "no."

Toad did the same.

We're not leaving until we figure this out.

"Hammer, Toad, is that you?"

Two clicks from Toad while William stood looking at the bed.

"We're coming to you."

Two more clicks from Toad, then they nodded at each other. William knew him like a twin brother and was sure they both were thinking the same thing.

We need to get this done on our own before the rest of them get here.

Toad shouldered his rifle, pointing it at the bed, while William let his dangle from the strap. Then, with both hands, he grabbed hold of the bed and yanked.

Despite the daily punishing workouts, it barely budged.

He's inside the bed!

With a firmer grip, William yanked and walked backward. The smell of the cologne strengthened.

The bed mumbled a curse.

After a few steps, a body fell onto the thickly carpeted floor.

The target let loose a string of Spanish swear words as he crawled slowly from under the bed and stood in the room.

5

WE FIGHT TO WIN

Alex "Axe" Southmark's Cabin
Rural Virginia

William smiled and shook his head. "This guy had hollowed out one side of the foam mattress into a space just his size, plus a little extra for breathing room. Can you believe that?"

"A hiding place no one would ever look for," Mad Dog said. "Except you."

"He must have heard one of the guards drop, or maybe we weren't as quiet as we thought we were. He had a warning and time to hide."

"But not shower," Mad Dog said. "Follow your nose—it always knows!"

Haley rolled her eyes and they all chuckled.

"Anyway, we cuffed him, took him in, and I got written up for a commendation because," he nodded at Mad Dog, "I followed my nose."

"Do we know him?" Nancy asked. "Would we recognize the name of the drug dealer?"

William shook his head. "I doubt it. It was a long time ago.

Besides, his people broke him out of prison a few days later. Or bribed the guards to let him go. Either way, he really did vanish after that."

"So it was all for nothing?" Haley asked.

"No," William said firmly. "We all got real-world experience on an actual mission. We proved that training pays off. And we caught the bad guy. What happens after we do our jobs is none of our business." He looked at each of them to emphasize the point. "We always do our best, no matter what."

After a few seconds, Axe quoted from the SEAL Ethos. "'We train for war and fight to win.'"

Everyone, warrior and analyst alike, raised their bottles in a toast and repeated the words. "We train for war and fight to win."

———

———

OPERATION WHITE FLAG

1

THE MISSION

Alex "Axe" Southmark's Cabin
Rural Virginia

Admiral William "Hammer" Nalen sat back after finishing his story and sipped his beer. It felt good to relive the old days. And hearing about how he and his Team had discovered the hiding drug dealer due to the smell of his cologne might someday help the men and women sitting in the cabin.

"One more?" Axe asked him.

The kid puts me on a pedestal, William thought, *but we're no different.*

Except Axe kept resisting his future.

He can't be a door-kicker forever. One of these days he's going to have to move out of the field and take on a bigger role.

The logs in the fireplace had burned down to embers. Axe's cabin felt cozy and filled with camaraderie. The intel side of their team got along with the direct-action personnel.

Haley's boss, Gregory, sat near his senior analysts, Nancy and Dave, on the couch.

Mad Dog and Axe sat in chairs across from them. Haley was the pivot point, sitting closest to the fire. Half analyst, half warrior.

As usual, William had chosen to sit near the kitchen, a few feet removed from the team. While he was one of the guys, he also carried the weight of making tough calls and sending people into harm's way.

Next to him, Mariana, the police officer from a small town in Texas, watched and listened with rapt attention.

I hope she makes it on the team.

He had a funny feeling about her but couldn't put his finger on what gave him pause.

Maybe I'm too set in my ways.

Mariana wasn't a SEAL—but then again, neither was Haley.

They'd give her a shot on an upcoming mission.

See what she's made of.

"Please, Hammer?" Haley said.

Nalen sipped his beer, shrugged his shoulders, and considered his options. Most of his stories were pretty boring compared with what Axe and Mad Dog had been through. They'd come up during a time of more action: conflicts in the Middle East, the War on Terror, and the continued War on Drugs. His direct-action days weren't very eventful —tons of training with the occasional exciting mission between.

Then he'd moved on to command—and those stories would surely put everyone to sleep.

"Okay, one more," he said. "Just remember, I didn't have two or three missions a night for years on end. I have fewer tales to pick from. But there's one about flexibility—and things going wrong," he said.

"A story where everything goes right isn't much of a story," Mad Dog pointed out. "'We went in, accomplished our mission, and got out' is pretty boring."

"True. But boring is our bread and butter," William said. "This was toward the end of my time on direct-action missions. I'd moved up and had gradually been tasked with more responsibility. Calling the shots. As you'll have to do someday soon, Axe," he said.

Axe shook his head and drank from his beer bottle but said nothing.

"So no shit, there I was," William said. "I can't tell you where, of course. There were sixteen of us, dropped off a long way from our target. We rarely had to travel so far, but the target had extensive lookouts. Flying in would be problematic—we'd be spotted and probably targeted by ground fire, rocket-propelled grenades, and even surface-to-air missiles. So we inserted, hiked all night, went to ground in the morning, and waited until nightfall, when we could hike the rest of the way," he said, remembering the sights and sounds of the jungle they'd spent so much time in. "A warlord and his gang had set up a camp in the middle of nowhere and were—supposedly—arming and training terrorists to hit the USA. We had to go in, get eyes on, and shake the tree."

"Sounds easy enough," Mad Dog said. "Been on dozens of those. Call in an airstrike if bad guys are found?"

William nodded. "If necessary. Taking them out quietly ourselves and recovering intel would be better."

"But riskier," Gregory muttered with an apologetic shrug. "Sounds like something the analysts would have pressed for, even if it made it harder and more dangerous for you and your guys."

"You got it," William admitted. "But we all know those intel people..." He smiled after a second to make sure Nancy, Dave, Gregory—and Haley—knew he was joking.

Mostly.

"What went wrong?" Axe asked. "Everything?"

"No, not at all. Just one. A kid with a white flag."

He took a sip of his beer and remembered.

2

THE FLAG

Many Years Earlier
The Jungle

The drop-off the previous night had gone flawlessly.

The hike through the jungle, while challenging physically and mentally, had been as expected. They'd had little intel on trails because of the extensive tree cover, but every member of the Team had plenty of experience by this time. Between the night vision goggles, endless hours of training in the heat and humidity of jungles like this one, and their conditioning, all fifteen of William's men—plus himself and an interpreter—were on task and moving forward.

It hadn't been dark long on the second night when they were up and moving. William was toward the rear of the column.

Step by careful step, the men snaked through the jungle, following the smallest game trails and natural openings. No bushwhacking here —they were in stealth mode.

Which made the sudden halt of the column surprising.

What's the holdup?

They were a few miles to the north of the area's main hamlet, which lay along a narrow stream, about a mile by canoe to the river.

They'd discussed inserting via the water, but intel didn't know the enemy's strength or detection abilities there, either. So they'd gone with the long hike in to be safe.

The local village had reportedly been forced to provide the warlord and his gang with food.

And, more troubling, young teen boys had been forced to join the man's army.

Villagers on downstream market runs had approached authorities and provided the initial intel about the warlord's activities. They wanted the warlord out and had been happy to report on the terrorist training camp deep in the jungle.

But William's Team had skirted the village for a reason—they didn't want any blowback on the locals from the operation he and his men were about to undertake. Nor did they want to confront any stray bad guys in the middle of civilians.

"Hammer and the 'terp up," came the quiet call over the radio.

This should be interesting.

William nodded his head to the interpreter, who looked like he didn't want to go anywhere near the front of the column. But William started forward, passing his men who'd faded into the trees on either side of the barely-there footpath, on alert and ready for action. The 'terp followed, not as quietly as a SEAL, but not pounding along like a civilian, either, thank goodness.

Seconds later, William saw a skinny boy, not more than ten years old, standing on the trail with his arms up. In one hand, he held a grimy, formerly white piece of clothing. A surrender flag.

Is that… underwear?

It looked like a pair of old, worn-out tighty-whities that had seen better days—if not years.

The point man had his M4 locked onto the boy, who wore torn shorts and a dark T-shirt at least a size too big for him. Both had a popular sports logo on them.

His family must have traded for those. Bet they were a birthday present—and are his prized possessions.

The people in the area were smart, resourceful, and had a surprising amount of connection to the outside world. Most every village, the intel people reported, had a television set, satellite dish, and a small generator to power it a few hours a night. Because everyone loves their sports.

William didn't bother to ask the point man any questions. Instead, he stepped forward, then to the side, and gestured behind him for the interpreter to jump in. "Quietly," is all he said.

The interpreter lowered himself to one knee, to be on the level of the boy's head, and whispered in the local dialect.

The boy chattered back quickly and efficiently, sounding like he was parroting a memorized speech more than having a conversation with the 'terp.

"The elders of the village to the south figured we'd come eventually," the 'terp translated. "There are kids on all the trails leading to the warlord's camp."

Behind William, the point guy must have been listening. "Didn't see him, sir. Damn near scared the crap out of me. Thought he was a ghost and almost lit him up at point-blank range. If it wasn't for the undies…"

"He and the others have been living out here, sleeping during the day and up all night, waiting for us to come," the interpreter continued after questioning the boy. "They get daily runner reports from the village."

"Why? What's going on?"

"The enemy has moved into the village. They're still training at the camp, but the men in charge prefer the comforts of civilization."

Or what passes for it around here, at least.

The kid, whose name was Jairo, spoke again—repeating carefully memorized sentences. "They are holding the village hostage. The bad guys figured we either wouldn't find them there or at least wouldn't drop a bomb on innocent civilians."

They're right about that.

"Okay. We call this in and see what command wants us to do."

"There's more, sir," the interpreter said. "The kid says the elders want us to attack… and he has a plan for us."

3

THE CALL

William accepted a fresh beer after a nod from Axe. This last one meant he'd be sleeping on the couch instead of driving home.

"Comm problems?" Mad Dog asked.

"Yep. Which left me making the decision," William said.

"All on the word of a child?" Nancy asked.

William shrugged. "He seemed legit. Serious. Very careful about what he said."

"Tough call," Axe muttered.

"Exactly. At a certain level, they all are."

"So what did you do?" Haley asked.

"We followed the kid."

"Into an ambush?" Mad Dog said, leaning forward.

"Well..."

Many Years Earlier
The Jungle

No one said a word, but William could sense the trepidation from a few of the guys. A ten-year-old kid ambushes them on the trail with a surrender flag made from someone's ancient white underwear and they follow him to the village?

"Don't translate anything I say," William said to the interpreter, "unless I'm talking directly to the kid. Even if he asks."

The 'terp nodded. No need to let a potential enemy in on the entire plan.

William split the Team in two. "You guys proceed to the camp," he said to the first eight men in the line. "Continue the mission. Figure out who is in the camp and what's going on. Take what the kid says with a grain of salt, but don't discount it." Jairo had told the interpreter all he knew about the operation from other kids sent to spy on it.

"Eliminate the bad guys, save any good guys or conscripts—especially the kids. Climb a tree or get to open ground if you need to call anything in. You know the drill. Get it done," he said to Harold—"Purple" or "Purp" for short—the man who would take charge of the smaller group. "Exfil as planned. We'll check out the village and either join up with you or exfil via the river."

Purp nodded once, gave his men a look, and headed out.

"The rest of us: buckle up. We're going for a ride."

The kid—Jairo—led the way. He moved through his jungle home as quietly as a SEAL and much more skillfully than the interpreter. As they neared the village, identified by the glow of a cooking fire through the thick trees and vines, the young man stopped and waited for the interpreter to come close.

"He says a man who shoots well should climb this tree," the 'terp said, pointing.

"Snipers?"

"He doesn't know that word," the interpreter explained, "but yes. That's what he means. A man up high enough will be able to shoot into the village at the bad men, he says."

William hesitated.

This isn't how we do things.

He wanted to recon the entire area. Set up snipers on overwatch wherever they thought best.

And not let a ten-year-old, or the elders who fed him these lines, dictate our attack.

A woman's scream carried faintly through the jungle. Jairo looked at him, the fear and worry mixed with resolve easily seen with William's NVGs. The cry made the decision easier and the situation more urgent.

We go with the villagers' plan... and hope it's not a trap.

"Get up that tree," he said to his remaining sniper. The man immediately started climbing.

It didn't take long. "Eyes on," he called over the radio. "In position. Clear shot to most of the vil except for the far right—west—side. There are fortifications every ten feet or so. They look like fighting positions."

"Copy."

Jairo explained the rest of the plan and the interpreter translated.

Not bad.

It gave William leeway to position his men where he wanted, but the intent was clear. They would approach from the east and lay off at the edge of the village clearing. Then they'd wait.

"He'll do what?" William asked the interpreter, though he'd heard the man clear enough.

"He'll run into the village and warn the tangos that you're coming. He says it's the only way he and his family survive if we aren't successful."

"Oh, we're going to succeed. Tell him that." He paused and looked at Jairo with understanding. "Wait. Ah, I get it." By announcing the imminent threat, all the bad guys would leave the huts and run to fighting positions.

At which point, we know who to kill.

William confirmed the second part of the warning with the kid—the bad guys would fight. The villagers would hide.

This will work.

A loud slap, followed by a sharp cry, cut through the hot, humid night from the village. They had to hurry.

"I want another shooter to the southeast in a tree," William said into the mic.

One of his men moved off into the jungle.

"And another in the bush on the north in case we're being set up or someone's bright enough to try to flank us. Everyone else: find good positions to the east of the village. Prepare to fire on any guys with weapons running to the prepared firing positions. Avoid ones looking reluctant to fight or hanging back—they might be villagers forced into it. Watch your targets and avoid shooting up the place."

He received clicks on the mics of the men in acknowledgment. Then they were off.

William caught the sight of Jairo through the trees as the kid ran through the jungle, no longer silent. As he neared the village, Jairo made the call of an animal—some kind of bird.

The kid's brave.

William just hoped it wasn't a setup. The trees and vines were much too thick to see any trip wires or other dangerous traps, especially once things got heavy.

We could be sitting ducks.

A few seconds later, the first tango burst through the door of one of the larger village huts. Then others emerged from various buildings, some groggy with sleep, others clearly drunk, but all well-armed and serious looking. They scrambled for the firing positions—low piles of tree branches and mud—and lay flat behind them.

Jairo kept up his run, straight into the largest building, where he let out another piercing cry.

The warning call for his people.

The villagers would be dropping to the ground—if they hadn't already—and taking cover.

"Open fire as targets present," William called out.

The snipers started picking off the tangos, then some of the SEALs with angles of fire on the bodies of the tangos joined in. The bad guys didn't know what had hit them. They were all dead in seconds, with the snipers doing most of the work.

"Kip—advance," William called to the man who had infiltrated close to the village on the north side. "Watch out for Kip entering the village," he added over the mic.

William lay on the damp ground. The snipers kept watch in the trees. And Kip slipped into the village like a ghost, so smoothly William didn't see him.

The *crack* of an unsuppressed shot came from the village—a pistol, William's mind immediately registered—followed an instant later by the return fire of a suppressed M4.

At least one tango had held back—and they'd got off a shot before Kip could.

4

THE COST

Alex "Axe" Southmark's Cabin
Rural Virginia

No one spoke in the cabin as William paused. The SEALs—along with Mariana and Haley—had all faced danger. William knew that Axe had taken over as a leader several times during missions. So had Mad Dog. But they'd never been in command of a large team, giving the orders— and hoping everyone made it out alive and unwounded.

Dealing with the consequences when it didn't go right.

"Kip?" Nancy asked softly in the near darkness of the cabin.

William didn't speak for a second.

"Jairo," Haley said, and William nodded.

William led his men through the jungle, on the lookout for tripwires or other dangers, though he found none.

"Main building is clear," Kip called over the radio, "and I didn't see any other tangos on the way in. But we've got one friendly down. Alive—for now."

The first feeling to hit William was relief. He hadn't lost Kip.

Then an overwhelming feeling of guilt flooded in.

He's just a kid.

"Snipers—any contacts?"

"No visible contacts."

"Copy. Kip: first aid on the friendly. Everyone else, clear buildings."

They got to work. The rest of the buildings were clear. Only the head honcho had stayed behind when the call came to fight.

"Dude had the gun on the kid as I came through the door, about to fire," Kip explained. His hands were covered in blood. Jairo's body looked small and frail in the bright light of Kip's headlamp, but Kip had managed to slow the bleeding. The boy's eyes were open, though his face was pale. "I wasn't fast enough."

"It's not on you," William said.

A short elder with the bearing of a proud man entered the hut, escorted by one of the SEALs. The villager and the interpreter started speaking rapidly.

"Jairo is his grandson. He wants to know if the boy will die," the 'terp translated.

"Kip?" William asked.

"Can we get a bird in here?"

"Doubtful," William said. There were still too many unknowns about the tango's operation. "But if we can get him in a boat and a bunch of miles downstream, I'll get a chopper to meet us. But we have to go now—and he might not make it." William nodded for the interpreter to translate.

Or the brass might say no.

Would a villager who helped them take out a bunch of criminals training terrorists be worth the risk of a helicopter? He wanted to believe the answer would be a solid "yes," but he couldn't be sure.

"You're in charge," William told Soapy, his second-in-command.

"I should go," Soapy argued as William carefully climbed into the narrow dugout canoe.

"Let me go, Hammer," Kip said, holding onto the stern of the small boat. Two shirtless, muscular villagers settled lightly into the fore and aft, holding wooden paddles, glaring impatiently at the SEALs.

"Meet up with the other guys, then get out. I've got this," William said. He had the radio, a spare med kit, but half his usual gear to make the boat as light as possible. Weight impacted speed—and every minute counted.

"Copy that," Soapy said. Kip nodded and gave the canoe a shove. Immediately, the men put their muscles to work, expertly guiding the boat into what little current the stream had and pulling for all they were worth.

5

THE STEP UP

"Jairo made it," William said.

No need to drag it out.

"The two men from the village about killed themselves paddling the canoe downriver. I called it in when I had coverage, and the brass agreed on an LZ they could live with. The chopper landed, I flew out with the kid, and he pulled through."

Everyone in the room let out a collective sigh of relief.

"What about your men?" Axe asked.

"Two wounded clearing the terrorist training camp. One seriously. But they accomplished the mission. Killed the warlord's men, killed the terrorists, rescued seven children and returned them to the village."

"All's well that ends well?" Mad Dog asked.

"In this case, yes. Not always, though," William said. But there was no need to bring the evening down with one of the stories where not everyone came home.

William caught Axe's eye. It was time for Axe to step up.

William's growing relationship with Senator Woodran meant he had to step back from the Team for a bit.

I just hope he's ready.

Axe had consistently resisted leaving behind the direct-action element of the business. He claimed he wasn't "management material."

I'll give him the news in the morning. Let him have one last night as a trigger-puller instead of an order-giver.

"Get this," William said. "Jairo is now the elder of the village." He shook his head in wonder at how the world turns.

"Nice story, Admiral," Nancy said with a warm smile.

"William. Or Hammer, please."

"Yes, sir."

Mad Dog held out his beer bottle. "To defending 'those who are unable to defend themselves,'" he said, quoting a part of the SEAL Ethos.

"And to all those who place the welfare and security of others before their own," Axe added, paraphrasing another one of the ethos lines.

They all clinked bottles, and William finished the last of his beer, thinking about the brave men he'd sent into battle who hadn't made it home… and wondering when the time would be up for the people in Axe's cabin.

OPERATION ONE SHOT

1

THE TEAM

The gathering in this story—and the next five—takes place immediately after the end of *A Team of Five*. Please read *A Team of Five* prior to these stories.

Alex "Axe" Southmark's Cabin
Rural Virginia

Stories had been shared. They had laughed together. Bonded.

Axe felt at home with these men and women—his new team. It wasn't the same as his fifteen-plus years as an active-duty SEAL, but nothing could take the place of that brotherhood. Still, these were good people.

There were the solid warriors: crazy, smart-ass Mad Dog. Shorter than average, with a barrel chest, bushy hair, and beard.

Tall, thin, graying Admiral Nalen, with his sharp mind and calm leadership.

And Haley, the young blond who had gone from office to operator in a year.

It wasn't the easiest or least traumatic way of learning, but "sink or swim" has its advantages.

On the other side of the small cabin's living room sat the intelligence analysts: Gregory, who had been quite the intel guy as a young man, from what Haley had said. Now his longish hair was going gray. He managed the team and had stepped into the role of handling the field assets.

Nancy, with her light flyaway hair especially frizzy from wearing a stocking cap, had embraced Haley's style of intel gathering and analysis. She'd helped save the day several times and, Haley had told him, seemed to have found a new lease on life—and on her career. She and Dave were definitely an item—they didn't hide it in the social setting of the team dinner. Dave, with his trimmed dark beard going more and more gray, was the most straitlaced of the group. He'd applied his incredible intellect to the intel and come through on several occasions.

Which left the newest member—or potential member—of the team: Mariana Rodriguez. A small-town Texas police officer with long dark hair, a round face, and a stocky, powerful physique.

Can we change her from a cop to an operator? And... should we?

Rodriquez was the most gung-ho potential operator he'd met, including the new SEALs he'd helped bring up over the years. But she had cop instincts, not those of a warrior.

And those could get her killed in battle.

"Well, it's about time to—" Axe started.

Mariana cut him off. "One more." She'd been silent all night except for the occasional laugh. "I need to hear all I can about what I'm getting into."

Axe nodded slowly but looked at Gregory. "You have time for another one? It's quick—I promise."

Gregory glanced at Nancy and Dave. They had made the trip together.

"One more," Gregory said.

Axe got a nod from the rest of the group. He knew exactly the story

Mariana needed to hear. Life as an operator differed greatly from that of a police officer. There were many similarities, but...

"It all starts with mindset," Axe said. "For example..."

He thought back to the time when he'd first made a name for himself—before he ever made it to his first Team.

"So no shit, there I was," he began. "A relatively new Navy SEAL at sniper school."

His body shuddered involuntarily, and he wondered if anyone noticed.

2

THE BEGINNING

Many Years Earlier
Navy SEAL Sniper Training Grounds
Somewhere in the United States of America

The training had been brutal. Alex—this was long before he would become known as "Axe"—was one of thirty students in the sniper program. From before dawn to after dusk every day, seven days a week, they shot, attended classroom training, and shot some more.

Eleven men had already vanished. One day, they were on the range and in the classroom. The next—after missing too many shots, or failing a classroom test—they were gone. No one talked about them, and Alex couldn't help but wonder what it would feel like to work so hard, to get so far, only to be sent back to the Team, where everyone would know you didn't make the cut.

It wouldn't happen to him.

While the others occasionally goofed off during rare moments of downtime, he didn't. He ate well, got to bed early, and stayed focused.

Like today. The sun beat down on him in his ghillie suit—a carefully constructed camouflage outfit that helped a sniper blend in perfectly with his surroundings. Alex sweated and moved forward another inch, slower than a turtle or snail.

In the distance, he had his target. But he was still a bit out of range. He had to move closer... and then wait. An instructor near the target scoped the dusty field with its sporadic rocks, brush, and shrubs, looking for Alex and three other students on the course as they snuck close enough for their sniper shots.

He had a twenty-minute time frame when his target would briefly appear in the window of a hut. Alex had to be in place, take the shot, and escape without being discovered. When his twenty-minute time was up, the next student—assigned to a slightly different section of the course—would be on.

Almost there. Another ten feet.

He froze. While he couldn't hear the quiet footsteps of an instructor near him, he could sense his presence and feel the tiniest tremor in the ground.

Damn it!

The man had to be nearly on top of him.

How did he get so close?

Alex froze and practiced a technique he'd started experimenting with. He shut down his mind, letting go of all thoughts and concerns. He didn't go dark—he was the darkness.

His body settled and relaxed into the ground.

He mostly closed his eyes, keeping them open only the tiniest amount. But unfocused—practically unseeing.

The instructor stopped only a few feet behind him.

Alex shut down... and disappeared.

3

THE CABIN

Alex "Axe" Southmark's Cabin
Rural Virginia

"At this point in the program," Axe explained to the group of men and women in the cabin, "being seen wouldn't be a failure. I wouldn't be sent home. But I didn't want to get caught. No matter what."

"No matter what..." Mad Dog muttered, nodding. "Sometimes, it's the principle of the thing."

"Exactly," Axe said.

"But there are also times it's a matter of life or death," Admiral Nalen said softly from near the kitchen.

Axe nodded. "And I knew that old saying, 'The more you sweat in training, the less you bleed in battle.' So I shut down and waited."

Many Years Earlier
Navy SEAL Sniper Training Grounds
Somewhere in the United States of America

The first few minutes felt like hours. He figured the instructor would wander away pretty quickly—then let the thought pass out of his mind. He had no attachments to time or the outcome. No tension. No energy to be picked up by a sensitive enemy, which is what the instructor was at that point.

Another thought flickered through his mind briefly.

Can he guess I'm here?

The instructor might be looking right at him, arms crossed with a huge grin on his face, letting him lay there and suffer when he'd already been caught.

He let it all go and returned to the darkness of invisibility.

A moment later, with his left cheek on the warm dirt, Alex saw an ant about eight inches away from his head—just close enough for his barely focused eyes to pick up.

It moved sideways across his vision before stopping. Its tiny antennae waved in the air for a second, then it turned toward Alex and seemed to regard him for a second.

It changed direction and walked directly at him.

Alex's eyes lost their clear view of it, but he could still track its movement.

He exhaled softly through his nose, hoping to scare it off, but the plan backfired.

Alex said a silent prayer as the ant crawled into his nostril.

THE NIGHTMARE

Alex "Axe" Southmark's Cabin
Rural Virginia

"No way. Stop. Time out," Nancy cried with a shudder. "I can't hear this," she added, her arms hugging herself. "I've hated ants since I was a little girl and sat on an ant hill. So… just…. no."

"Sorry," Axe said with a laugh. "I can fast-forward to the end if you want."

"No!" Mad Dog said. "I have to know. And it would be good for Mariana to hear, right?"

Axe shrugged and looked at Nancy, who took a long drink of her beer. "Fine. Go ahead. But keep the descriptions to a minimum, if you can."

He nodded, betting she was going to have nightmares later.

Then he had a sip of his own beer. "Remember, it's all about mindset," he explained to Mariana.

Many Years Earlier
Navy SEAL Sniper Training Grounds
Somewhere in the United States of America

The little bugger tickled as it wandered into his nostril, hung out for a few seconds, then walked back out.

Alex's shield slipped for an instant as the ant climbed the outside of his nose and meandered toward his eyes. He closed them tight and focused on not changing his slow, light breathing.

One ant will not make me give up and reveal myself.

He settled back into the zone.

This too shall pass.

With his eyes tightly closed, he didn't see the ant's buddies approach, but he felt them. One by one, they entered his nostrils, explored, and exited. Some tiptoed across his lips. Others crawled on his face. More followed their scout over his eyes and into his hair.

There's nothing wrong with ants.

They weren't biting him, at least. Just exploring.

The instructor moved a step closer.

That's when Alex felt the first ants on his legs.

Alex "Axe" Southmark's Cabin
Rural Virginia

The entire team in the cabin stared at Axe.

Nancy's mouth was fixed in a grimace of horror.

Mad Dog grinned, his eyes wide—he loved the story.

Nalen looked at Axe with what Axe took as pride.

The others were a combination of fascinated and repulsed.

"They found openings in my clothes. I don't know how, but they did. It was… interesting," he said.

The understatement of the year.

"But I refused to quit."

Many Years Earlier
Navy SEAL Sniper Training Grounds
Somewhere in the United States of America

The ants covered his arms, legs, back, and head, including his face. Alex's focus slipped. He was no longer darkness—invisible. He was just a young guy laying on or near an anthill, quickly going crazy.

His breathing picked up and his body rebelled, followed by his mind. Every ounce of his being wanted—needed—to jump up, strip off his ant-covered clothes, and kill the tiny invaders on his skin.

I will not give up.

He'd made it through BUD/S training. He'd suffered the cold water of the Pacific Ocean at all hours of the day and night. He had run, crawled, and rolled in the sand until he chafed in places no man wanted to chafe.

He hadn't given up then…

And he wouldn't now.

An ant on his earlobe finally had the idea to sample the flesh it was walking on. A second later, they were all biting him.

Earlier, the seconds had felt like hours. Now, each felt like days.

His resolve faltered instantly.

I will never quit.

The short mantra had kept him going through the darkest times of Hell Week, the culmination of the first part of SEAL training.

I will never quit.

He kept repeating it in his mind, but the conviction behind it, and the power he got from thinking it, diminished with every sharp bite from the hundreds?—thousands?—of ants crawling all over his body.

Eating me.

He felt like he would go crazy if he didn't get the ants off him.

But he held on.

Another ten seconds.

Alex counted.

Ten seconds later, he repeated the phrase, and counted again.

To his right and a few steps behind him, the instructor made a strange noise. Part surprise, part disgust.

"Oh, hell no," the man muttered, followed by what sounded like him hitting his pant legs.

"What the...?"

A second later, he walked off in a hurry, retreating from the area.

Now.

With the same slow, careful movements as earlier, Alex edged forward a few inches, paused for ten seconds, then edged to his left. A shallow gulley, barely four inches deep, might shield him from view of the instructor a few hundred yards to the front—if he could get there before losing control.

The ants kept crawling and biting. Each seemed intent on sampling as many different parts of his flesh as they could.

Alex kept his eyes closed. The ants in and out of his nostrils were bad enough. He didn't need them crawling over his eyeballs, too.

After several excruciating minutes, he slid into the shallow ditch and took a risk. His hands moved in slow motion to avoid attracting the eye of not only the instructor in front but any others wandering around nearby. He swept his face first, knocking the ants from his eyelids and lips, then digging them out of his nose.

Next, he rolled slowly onto his back and squirmed, all as slowly as possible. His hands pressed against his skin, killing the ants inside his clothing and the ones outside trying to get in.

They died by the hundreds. Others left of their own volition. Some remained, but Alex could deal with them.

He got his mind right and, inch by inch, rolled onto his stomach.

One inch at a time, he continued forward, closing the distance so he could take his shot.

5

THE ANSWER

Alex "Axe" Southmark's Cabin
Rural Virginia

"I don't know if I crawled through an anthill or if they were just out hunting—or whatever ants do," Axe said. "But I survived, nailed my shot, and eventually graduated."

Someday I'll tell them other stories from sniper school.

He later perfected his "going dark" technique and made a name for himself by surprising an instructor. But that was a story for another night.

Axe checked on Nancy, who looked relieved the story was over.

He saw the resolve on Mariana's face, and his opinion of her went up yet another notch.

"Mindset," she said.

Axe nodded. "Mindset."

After a few seconds, Admiral Nalen spoke from near the kitchen, "The question is, how long could you have stuck it out? If the instructor hadn't left—or you had been in enemy territory?"

Axe nodded. "That is the question."

And we both know the answer.

If necessary, he would have let his body get eaten alive before giving up.

I will never quit.

OPERATION WHITE STRIPE

1

THE CABIN

With dinner finished, it was Axe's favorite time. The after-mission get-togethers were always a great time to tell stories, bond with teammates, and work through the emotions that came from being at the tip of the spear—running and gunning, protecting the country, and saving lives.

The fire burned brightly, throwing off light and welcome warmth on the cool spring evening.

Closest to the fire, on the couch and comfortable chairs, sat the intelligence team from the Central Analysis Group.

Haley looked relaxed and at peace—a welcome change.

She's letting go of some of the challenges she's faced—that's good to see.

She kept pushing her long blond hair behind her ears, though it slipped forward again minutes later.

Gregory looked less comfortable, but he still smiled and participated.

It might be tough for him, being the boss yet hanging out with the troops.

Next time, Axe would pull a chair over for Gregory to sit near the kitchen, next to him, to create some separation and distance, which would probably help.

Nancy hung on every word of each story, living vicariously through the warriors.

Did she ever want to get into the field? A team-building exercise at a gun range might be fun for everyone.

Dave fit right in but didn't say much, just like Marcus—an analyst Haley respected from her office.

Dave has more gray than ever in his beard. I guess we're all growing older—and the stress of the job doesn't help any of us.

Across from the couch and chairs were the operators. Mad Dog cracked jokes, as always. Johnboy smiled and relaxed, as patient and solid as ever.

Mariana was there too, with her long, straight dark hair hanging free instead of up in its usual tight bun. She wasn't an official member of the group yet.

She could be a welcome addition—if she can handle it.

Admiral Nalen was the only one missing—off working with Senator Woodran. He was missed.

"Johnboy, we haven't heard any stories from you," Axe said. He didn't know nearly enough about the quietest member of the group.

The dark-skinned, muscular man with close-cropped black hair grinned. "Me? I don't have any stories. I go in and get the job done. Thankfully, nothing much spectacular or exciting has happened. Just, you know, taking care of business."

Axe nodded but waited him out.

Everybody has stories.

JB sighed. "Okay, one. But here's a warning," the big man said, his face and voice stern. "There will be no new nicknames for me. 'Johnboy' or 'JB' are fine. Agreed?"

Axe nodded with the others around the room.

Mad Dog chuckled next to Johnboy. He must have heard the story before.

"And you—nothing out of you," Johnboy said. His tone was as

serious as ever, but his eyes sparkled and lips twitched, fighting to hold off a smile. Mad Dog and Johnboy had become fast friends in their most recent adventures.

"Okay, okay. You don't have to 'odor' me around," Mad Dog said.

Johnboy let out an exaggerated sigh. "See, that's what I'm talking about." He turned to the rest of the group. "Have you heard the story about Axe's old team lead—Red—in the helicopter?

Haley had, but none of the others knew the story.

"Operation Deadly Silence," Axe said, cluing in the rest of the team. "But we're not telling that one tonight. You have to hear it directly from him."

"Absolutely," Johnboy agreed. "I only bring it up because my story has similarities." He took a sip of his beer and shook his head. "I can't believe I'm going to tell you all this, but here goes. So no shit, there I was. I can't tell you where, of course. And in my defense, I'd been awake for over seventy-two hours at that point."

Then he stared at the fire, remembering.

2

THE MOUNTAINS

Many Years Earlier
The High Jungle

The part of the country where Johnboy and the three men of his fireteam found themselves was mountainous and covered with what seemed like every type of green plant in the world, growing close together. It was wetter than a forest but not quite a typical jungle. Lots of fog and rain made it lush, beautiful, and exceedingly difficult to traverse.

JB was on point again, leading the way silently through the thick foliage. Ahead, just at the edge of his hearing, the soft noises made by the men they were following stopped.

Instantly, JB raised his arm, fist clenched.

His Team froze on the narrow game trail behind him.

They can't see or hear us—we're too good.

Still, the bad guys frequently paused.

Could be they're checking the map or taking a break.

It didn't mean they suspected they were being followed.

With any luck, we're going to stop soon.

Nearly seventy-two hours earlier, the SEALs had been in the right place at the right time. A small four-wheel-drive pickup, battered and muddy, had pulled to a stop at the edge of the forest. Through their night vision goggles, the men had watched it climb the steep mountain dirt road, up switchback after switchback.

For once, the intel had been correct.

Four men had climbed out of the truck's open bed, struggled to shoulder large, heavy backpacks, and started up the trail.

If the rest of the intel was right, the men would lead the SEALs to a well-hidden drug lab deep in the mountains. The local government and the United States had long been hunting for it. But because of the mountains, the silence of the locals—paid well by the local drug cartel to keep their mouths shut—and the tree cover, none of the methods to discover the location had worked.

So the SEALs had been sent in.

Johnboy had led the way the first night. The backpacks likely contained supplies—raw materials needed by the drug lab and food for the workers there.

Because of the heaviness of the packs and the difficult terrain, following the slow-moving men hadn't been difficult at first.

But the local drug mules knew the pathways and had likely made the trip before.

The Americans hadn't.

Near dawn, the sounds of the men moving in front of them stopped, replaced by quiet conversation.

What happened next didn't become clear until several minutes later. As the men continued moving—after only a minute of rest—JB and the Team followed… and almost gave themselves away.

The original four men who had walked through the night relaxed in a clearing.

The heavy backpacks were gone.

But the sounds of a small group of men moving through the woods continued.

3

THE UNDERGROUND

"The enemy handed off the packs?" Axe asked, guessing what had happened.

Johnboy nodded. "We're still not sure why. It might have been so they were harder to track. Or to destroy the will of anyone following. Or just to get the supplies in—and drugs out—as quickly as possible."

"So you were still following four guys—just not the same four?" Nancy asked.

JB nodded again. "At that point, we realized we were following the backpacks, not the men."

"How long did that go on?" Dave asked quietly.

Johnboy chuckled. "Too long."

Many Years Earlier
The High Jungle

The second set of four men walked all day, following narrow game trails up and down the mountains.

The SEALs trailed behind, stopping only when their targets stopped—which wasn't often or for long. But they were able to drink and even eat a few energy bars. Plus, they were SEALs, trained for adversity and unwilling to quit.

After twelve hours on the move, the men ahead slowed... then stopped in another tiny clearing. Quiet words were exchanged with four more waiting men. The backpacks were shrugged off and turned over to the new guys, who immediately left the clearing and continued along the narrow trail.

The SEALs followed, starting their second twenty-four hours of marching.

After four more hand-offs, Johnboy and the Team were running on fumes.

Could they know we're here?

He'd been awake for over three days. On his feet—following the backpacks up and down mountains—for seventy-two hours. He had only communicated with the Team through hand signals but he could tell, just by glancing at them, they were as tired as him.

The intel is always wrong.

They'd never give up, but... could the drug cartel have known about the mission? Were the men with the backpacks leading them on a wild goose chase for fun—or drawing them in, far from help, for an ambush?

This is stupid. Who puts a drug lab this far into the mountains, anyway?

In the gathering dusk, JB made eye contact with Will—call sign "Wilbur." With gestures, JB confirmed Wilbur knew where they were on the map and signed that they had to be close to the end of the march.

The sounds from ahead changed.

They're putting down the backpacks.

Without the heavy packs, the men moved quietly. Not as silently as SEALs—but definitely like men with experience in nature.

They're spreading out—and doing a backcountry version of a surveillance detection routine.

The four drug mules would likely stalk the area for signs they were being tailed.

JB signaled and his men faded into cover.

Johnboy sensed more than heard one of the tangos walk within five feet of him.

If it were fifteen minutes earlier—and lighter—the man might have seen JB hidden in the foliage. But at this time of night, just after dusk in the mountains, he had no hope of detecting the experienced SEAL.

The tango walked right by.

Several minutes later, Johnboy crept forward just in time to see—in the green glow of his night vision goggles—the tangos manhandle the heavy packs through a gap in the trees… and disappear.

Where the hell did they go?

4

THE SILENCE

"We couldn't hear them anymore," Johnboy explained to the men and women in Axe's cabin, "so we figured they'd gone underground."

He took a much-needed sip of beer. "We were all pretty done at that point. We'd never quit or give up, of course, but that doesn't mean we were having the time of our lives. We were annoyed at the intel geeks for sending us on this chase and pissed at the tangos for dragging our asses up and down the mountains. All we wanted was to finish the mission and sleep for a few days."

"But?" Nancy asked.

"We'd been given wide latitude on the mission," he explained. "Ideally, the local government wanted it to be their operation. We were supposed to call in the location of the drug lab, keep an eye on the situation, and wait for their people to trek in and handle it."

"But with the distance and time that would take..." Axe said from his chair close to the kitchen.

"Exactly," Johnboy agreed. "That, plus being hot, sweaty, and tired, made it an easy choice. We decided to raid it ourselves."

Many Years Earlier
The High Jungle

The SEALs were in agreement: no calling in the location and waiting for days while the local government sent troops in by foot or risked trying to lower them from helicopters through the thick tree canopy. Cutting out the middleman made all the sense in the world.

But first, we give the enemy a chance to settle in—and ourselves time to rest.

Johnboy silently directed his men to overwatch positions and worked out a rest schedule. He took the first watch shift, found a comfortable spot to lay down, and carefully surveyed the area around where the tangos had vanished.

It's a good place to ambush us.

The small game trail they'd been following meandered into a flat clearing. A thick grove of trees on the far side likely concealed the entrance to an underground drug lab.

We would have heard the men leave the trees, even without the packs.

JB and his men could approach from the sides or back, but they might miss the entrance to the lab. Better to wait a while.

First rest. Then recon.

And surely there had to be sentries in the area, right?

They could be relying on how remote and hidden the place is.

JB stayed alert but calmed his body, waiting for whatever came next.

An hour later, it happened.

Johnboy's watch was up. He could quietly grab a snack, drink more water, and get some much-needed sleep while one of his teammates took over.

But he'd been so still and quiet for so long, the jungle had grown used to him and determined he wasn't a threat. Critters moved around nearby—tiny noises in the darkness—unseen for the most part. But ahead, coming along the game trail toward him, JB saw an adorable, white-striped squirrel, easy to make out in the green of his night vision goggles.

As a child in New York City—and later upstate New York—he'd seen his share of squirrels. The brownish gray ones were most common, of course, even in the big city.

Upstate, he'd been surprised the first time he saw an all-black squirrel.

On a family vacation to Colorado, he'd seen a red squirrel.

But I've never seen one like that with a white stripe.

5

THE SQUIRREL

Alex "Axe" Southmark's Cabin
Rural Virginia

Johnboy paused, waiting to see if the incredibly smart people in the room caught on before he filled in the rest of the details.

Mad Dog kept his mouth shut, as promised. Everyone else looked like they wanted to ask but weren't sure what to say.

Finally, Nancy spoke up. "I've never heard of squirrels with white stripes." Her brows furrowed in confusion. "The only animal with a white stripe I can think of is—" She stopped, eyes widening.

"Oh, no," Haley muttered.

"Oh, yes!" Mad Dog giggled like a little kid, no longer able to contain himself.

"Yes," Johnboy agreed. "But I hadn't put it together yet. Remember, between prepping for the mission and waiting for the tangos to show, then following them through the mountains, I'd had about three hours of sleep in the previous four days. It wasn't quite Hell Week at BUD/S, but it was close."

Many Years Earlier
The High Jungle

Johnboy didn't want to move and startle the creature, causing it to scamper away noisily, so he froze.

Walk on by, little buddy.

The animal came closer, nose to the ground, sniffing.

The head looks different from the other squirrels I've seen. The body, too.

Once the mission was done and he was home from deployment, he'd have to mention it to his dad. The man had a love-hate relationship with squirrels. On the one hand, Dad loved to watch them beneath the bird feeder, chowing down the seeds tossed aside by the birds above.

But when the "damn rodents!"—as Dad called them—managed to leap onto the freestanding bird feeder, he rapped on the window and tried to scare them off. Then he'd move the feeder further away from whatever the squirrels had jumped from.

The animal in front of Johnboy stopped and raised its nose to smell the air. Maybe JB had made the slightest noise or the light breeze had shifted, carrying his scent.

The squirrel knew something was nearby that shouldn't be.

Something dangerous.

In a flash, it spun and raised its tail.

The breeze shifted again, carrying with it the telltale smell, which hit Johnboy's nose at the same time his mind put the pieces together.

That's not a squirrel—it's a skunk!

He didn't move much—only lowered his face to the ground—but it was enough to complete the fear circuitry in the skunk's tiny brain. It sprayed the danger behind it—then ran.

6

THE OWLS

Alex "Axe" Southmark's Cabin
Rural Virginia

Johnboy shook his head slowly, remembering that night.

"You know, I thought I smelled something earlier," Mad Dog said. "But I didn't want to say anything."

"Hilarious, my friend."

"It got you?" Nancy asked.

"Absolutely," Johnboy said. "Thankfully, I was laying down, but it settled on me just fine. And it stank like you wouldn't believe."

Many Years Earlier
The High Jungle

Johnboy could barely stand the smell.

Assuming we get out of this damn place alive, the guys will never let this go.

As a child, a neighbor's dog had gotten sprayed by a skunk. The smell had lasted weeks, no matter what the family did. JB couldn't remember all the things they tried to clean the poor pup, but one thing stuck in his mind.

The first few minutes are the most important.

If the oily residue is removed quickly, it's easier to neutralize and doesn't last as long.

Unfortunately, he was a seventy-two-hour hike away from remedies that might help—shampoo, baking soda, tomato juice—or a shower.

Outside of Hell Week at BUD/S, there hadn't been many times when he'd needed to use one of the more memorable Navy SEAL sayings to keep himself motivated. But this certainly qualified.

Embrace the suck.

Take the horrible situation and welcome it—that was the way to get through anything the world threw at you.

Since there was nothing else he could do, he would embrace the experience.

He drank some water, had a snack, closed his eyes, and slept.

Hours later, the hardest part for the other three men of Johnboy's Team was not giving away their position by laughing at his predicament.

But they had a job to do—and it was 3 a.m. The perfect time to attack.

JB took the far left flank on the approach, skirting several feet farther over than he normally would to keep from making his teammates' eyes water with his scent.

Woooo-woooo-wooo.

What sounded like the low-pitched call of a bird—an owl, maybe —came from ahead.

Skunks are natural prey for owls.

Great—now he had to avoid being a target for—

That wasn't an owl.

Johnboy stopped. His Team stopped with him, coming to the same conclusion he had.

That's a person who caught my scent—and doesn't want a skunk anywhere near them. They're imitating the call of an owl to scare it off.

The sound came again, but JB still couldn't make out a person—or owl—in the dense woods.

He took one step closer.

Woooo-woooo-wooo.

Johnboy narrowed down the location and took his time, examining every branch.

There.

In the green glow of the NVGs, JB could barely make out a rifle barrel poking around a tree.

Shifting right, Johnboy trusted his Team to flow with him as he stepped to the side, away from the hidden sentry.

After a few more minutes of stealth, another call came from in front of him.

Woooo-woooo-wooo.

7

THE OVERWATCH

Alex "Axe" Southmark's Cabin
Rural Virginia

Johnboy waited again for his new team to put the pieces together.

Dave got there first this time. "The enemy gave themselves away?"

JB nodded. "We drifted around and scoped them all out. Very carefully disguised and hidden. We might have seen them before it was too late…" He trailed off.

"But if you had called it in," Haley said, "the host-country's army guys probably wouldn't have."

He nodded. "It would have been a bloodbath. They had guys all over."

"But they weren't expecting SEALs," Axe said quietly.

Exactly.

"It was pretty easy after that," Johnboy said. "We picked our targets. Took out the ones farthest from the drug lab first—quietly."

"You helped?" Nancy asked.

He shook his head. "I was on overwatch—downwind!" He grinned. "After we took care of the drug lab, we exfilled a different way than we came in. Turns out we were only about an eight-hour walk from another trailhead—that's how they normally got their supplies in and drugs out. The forced march was for our benefit only."

"The intelligence is always wrong," Axe muttered with an apologetic look to the men and women of the Central Analysis Group.

"Actually, no," JB said, correcting Axe. "The intel was right—the truck, the trailhead, the men with the backpacks. But it turns out there was a traitor in the host country's intelligence division. Surviving the ambush and getting out of the mountains quickly allowed us to notify our people, who worked some sort of sting. Took down a bunch of corrupt guys and likely saved a lot of lives in the long run."

"How long did the smell last?" Nancy wanted to know.

"Three weeks. And every now and then, I swear I can smell it on me still." He raised his beer. "The only easy day was yesterday."

The entire team toasted and drank.

"No new nicknames at all?" Mad Dog asked.

Johnboy shook his head sternly, his eyes narrowed. There had been plenty once the Team had gotten back to base. With his strong "encouragement," they hadn't taken root. "None."

He waited for Mad Dog to needle him, but surprisingly, the man just nodded.

"Fine," Mad Dog sighed. "But that really stinks."

The team groaned and rolled their eyes.

JB just smiled, relaxed in the warmth of the fire, and waited for the next story.

OPERATION FIRST KILL

1

THE RIGHT CALL

Alex "Axe" Southmark's Cabin
Rural Virginia

The stories rolled on as the fire slowly died. Axe got another round of beers for everyone, turning off the kitchen lights, leaving the cabin's living room lit only by the fading fire and a few lamps.

Ty "Johnboy" Johnson sat quietly, a relaxed smile on his face. He'd entertained them earlier with the story of his encounter with a "white-striped squirrel," but he'd only listened and laughed since.

Haley sat on the couch, head tilted back, looking like she was half asleep. Her long blond hair seemed to glow in the dim light from the fire.

The rest of the team from the Central Analysis Group enjoyed the stories, but Axe felt an undercurrent. It took him a few minutes to put his finger on it, but it came together eventually.

They don't have exciting stories to tell, Axe thought. *Or they think they don't.*

The analysts dealt with Top Secret data that likely couldn't be shared with mere trigger-pullers, but he vowed to give the intel team space to share whatever they could.

There have to be stories they can tell. Probably not as exciting or dangerous as ours, but still. Terrorist cells they stopped with timely research, holes in security they helped fix—something.

Gregory, with his fashionable glasses and longer-than-regulation gray hair neatly held in place with what must be a ton of hair product, had been in the business for decades.

I wonder what he's seen.

Instead of speaking, Gregory only smiled encouragingly and laughed in all the right places.

Nancy, her hair frizzy from the stocking caps she wore three seasons of the year, hung on every story and asked great questions.

Dave, her boyfriend—though it wasn't talked about, it was clear as day they were a couple—drank his beers and seemed to take the descriptions of some of the warriors' antics with a hefty grain of salt.

Smart man.

Axe knew little about Marcus, the newest analyst to join their group, but he looked smart, well put together, and had helped save lives during the most recent mission, which made him all right in Axe's book.

Admiral Nalen was off working with Senator Woodran, but sitting near the fire was Doug "Mad Dog" McBellin—short, burly chested, hairy—more like a small bear than a man.

In the lull following the latest story, the newest member of the team spoke up. "I have a question," Mariana started.

The serious look on her face told Axe the night was about to turn from fun stories to an important discussion.

Here we go. Leave it to Tex to dive in and get real.

"Don't get me wrong," Mariana continued. "The stories are great and all, but..." She hesitated and looked at the fire.

"Say it," Axe said. "You can ask us anything."

Mad Dog leaned forward with a grin, ready to offer a suggestion about what was—and wasn't—off-limits, but Axe silenced him with a sharp shake of his head.

Mariana looked from Haley to Mad Dog, then to Johnboy, before finally asking Axe, "When do you know to pull the trigger and kill someone?"

The question hung in the room.

The analysts shifted uncomfortably.

Axe didn't have to look at his fellow warriors—including Haley—to know they, too, had switched their gazes to a thousand-yard stare as memories flooded in.

He had killed his share of people.

He'd also elected not to kill a few.

Usually, the enemy you let live was the enemy you had to fight again. But there were exceptions to every rule. There was the operator in Los Angeles that he'd held at gunpoint—and let go.

He wondered where she was right then—and if he'd made the right call.

2

THE PRIORITIES

Sortavala, Russia

Ekaterina woke with a start, her eyes snapping open. She expected to see someone in the room, ready to kill her—or worse—but she was alone in the tiny cabin.

A hint of color shined in the dawn sky through her window.

The Russian operator and assassin took a deep breath, calming herself. She ran her hands through her short brown hair—dyed—brushing the bangs out of her eyes, and felt old.

I'm safe. I made it through another night.

More than a week had passed since she had fled America without reporting to Moscow.

What do they think happened to me?

She guessed the intelligence division was still putting the pieces together from her failed mission.

They may think I got shot and am lying dead somewhere.

It seemed farfetched, but she could hope. No matter what, however, she had another day to live. To do anything she wanted, free from orders sending her to spy, steal, or kill.

Like in the dream...

She had dreamed—again—of her first mission.

I'm not getting out of bed quite yet.

She closed her eyes and remembered that day. So there she was…

Many Years Earlier

Moscow, Russia

Ekaterina had been at the spy school for four years, since a few days after her parents died in a car accident. With no other living relatives, the authorities had taken one look at her stellar grades, athleticism, and grit before announcing she would go to a special school where she would learn a trade to be of service to her country.

She was bullied from day one. At ten, she had been three years younger than the next youngest student.

It only took sending three of the older girls who bullied her to the infirmary before the rest backed off.

Now, at fourteen, it was finally time to prove her abilities outside of the school environment. Protecting the younger girls from bullying was one thing. Succeeding on her first mission, out in the real world, was completely different.

"You will be nervous," Igor said.

Igor almost certainly wasn't his real name. None of the instructors or students used their real names at the school. She was called Katya, which was close enough to Ekaterina for her tastes. Her parents had called her Kat, as did all her friends. Or they had, before she'd been plucked from her old life and thrust into this one. And while she didn't exactly have friends here—they were comrades and also competitors—they called her Kat as well.

As much as Igor thought she'd be nervous, she didn't feel it yet. She was curious, excited even, but mostly she just wanted to get it over with. She was one of the last in the group of fourteen-year-olds to get a real training assignment. The other girls held it over her, looking down on her lack of experience—at least in their eyes.

As if one mission made them experts.

"Nervous is good," Igor continued. He finished tying a white ribbon in her pale blond hair. The ribbon matched her white, ankle-length dress. The shoes Igor had given her fit well, but the low heel and buckle of the white Mary Janes felt foreign. All her training had been done either barefoot on the fighting mats or in thick soled combat boots. She didn't relish having to do anything more strenuous than walking in these ridiculous shoes.

The outfit made her look like an innocent girl, which she hated, but it was the perfect disguise for the mission. With her short stature, the men wouldn't see a fourteen-year-old spy in training. They would think of her as a ten- or twelve-year-old lost little girl looking for her daddy.

With her parents dead, playing the part wouldn't be difficult.

"You remember the mission priorities?" Igor asked.

"Priority 1," she recited from memory, "confirm the presence of the targets." She had memorized the faces of three men who should be at the meet, along with a dozen others who might be there.

"Priority 2: if possible, without arousing suspicion, get a glimpse of the file folders and papers that should have come from a briefcase and may be out in the open."

"And?" Igor said, straightening the bow a final time and pushing himself up, his knees creaking. He was an old man, with gray hair, tired eyes, and a stale smell.

"Steal the papers and briefcase if an opportunity presents itself."

Igor stiffened as the door to the dressing room opened. Kat shifted her weight and clenched her right hand, using her index finger to fiddle with her thumb, perfectly playing the part of a nervous young girl.

"What do you think?" Igor asked Masha, the assistant director of the school and the person in charge of this mission.

With her sour face pinched in an ever-present frown, Masha stopped in front of Kat and looked her up and down. Eventually, she nodded slowly. "Good. And what is last priority, young lady?"

She must have been listening at the door this whole time—or the room is bugged.

"Get away."

Kat didn't see how she'd accomplish any more than her primary objective of observing the men in the room. Getting away safely after that seemed easy enough. It would only be a problem if she attempted to steal the papers.

They hadn't told her why the files in the briefcase were important, of course, but they wouldn't send her on a mission if they weren't valuable. And since they had to be valuable, the men would pay attention and notice immediately if she took them—or looked at them too closely.

Unless…

"Will there be a distraction to allow me to take the papers?" she asked.

"Well done, Katya," Igor said. "There will be a distraction, but it can't be large or it will backfire, causing them to be immediately suspicious. We walk a fine line. But don't worry. You do your part. We will take care of the rest," he said, his voice ice cold.

Sortavala, Russia

Ekaterina stared at the ceiling of the tiny cabin before forcing herself out of bed. She needed tea—or vodka. Something to wet her mouth. Just thinking about skinny fourteen-year-old Kat in that perpetually cold warehouse on the outskirts of Moscow—which served as their home, school, and training grounds—made her mouth dry.

She put the kettle on the stove, stoked the nearly dead coals in the fireplace, and added kindling. When it caught, she stacked larger logs on top. The cabin would heat up quickly despite the cold spring air outside.

When the water boiled, she poured it over her tea, forgoing her usual toast-and-jam breakfast. After all these years, she knew enough not to eat while remembering her first mission.

3

THE MISSION

Many Years Earlier
Moscow, Russia

There was a great deal of debate among the girls. Some claimed the missions were real. Completely authentic.

Others insisted it was all just play-acting, scenarios designed to test the girls in a controlled environment and staffed with former and current operators, trustworthy people who could act well and not give themselves away.

Kat didn't care. She just wanted to do a great job and stop the incessant teasing about the delayed timing of her first mission.

And still her own concerns that she wasn't good enough.

She knocked timidly on the glass door of the restaurant. Her thumb flicked against her finger, just the way she had practiced.

The door cracked open. A huge man in a tight suit—a bodyguard—stuck his head out. It was tiny compared with his body. He looked up and down the block, but no one else was on the sidewalks at the moment.

"Let her in," a man's voice called.

The guard narrowed his eyes at her but must have bought the young, harmless girl act. He opened the door, and she stepped hesitantly inside the restaurant.

"Is my father here?" she asked in her best little girl voice. She glanced around quickly. The restaurant was deserted except for two men at a table near the back. They shuffled papers into folders, turning away from her to hide their actions.

Kat let her shoulders sag at the sight of the empty room, but inside she was thrilled.

I've accomplished my mission.

She'd glimpsed the "Top Secret" labels on the folder—in English —before the men hid them.

The three men were exactly the ones she had been told to expect.

The oldest one—about the same age as her father would have been— walked close and knelt on one knee to be face-to-face with her. "Who's your father?" he asked. He didn't look suspicious—just concerned.

He's a father himself and understands how scared I am.

"He eats lunch here," Kat said in a trembling voice.

Igor had been right—she was nervous and must have looked it.

The man smiled kindly and gestured at the restaurant. "It's closed today. He's not here."

"I'm sorry," she whispered, her voice filled with disappointment. "I'll go to the bar."

The bar was the next obvious place for her fictitious father.

Now all I have to do is leave without arousing suspicion.

That's when the mission went to hell.

On the street outside, a car's horn.

Skidding tires.

The crash of metal on metal nearby.

The distraction!

Instead of causing the men to hurry to the windows to check out the accident on the quiet side street, all four men drew guns from beneath their jackets.

And the crashing car triggered something inside her.

My parent's accident…

She forced down those feelings. If she thought about that, she wouldn't survive the next few minutes.

Before she could run, the fatherly man snaked his arm around her and jabbed the gun against her temple. He backed away from the door, following the two from his table as they hurried to the far corner of the restaurant.

She could smell the man's fear.

In a moment, she knew the answer to the debate at school about the missions.

No one can act that well. This isn't a training exercise. This is real.

The accident, meant to be a distraction, had instead made the men immediately suspicious.

And she was now a hostage.

4

THE TUNNEL

Many Years Earlier
Moscow, Russia

The man's two companions rushed to the rear of the restaurant. He dragged her to a doorway, walking backward, intent on the front door.

They reached a staircase leading down to the basement.

The men thought they were about to be attacked and had planned an escape.

They don't realize it's only me.

Or was it? Could there be another part to the mission she didn't know about? More operators standing by, kept secret from her so she wouldn't reveal anything given her youth and inexperience?

The front door didn't crash in. The burly guard there with the pistol in his hand stood ready... but nothing happened.

The man half-carried her small body down the first few stairs. The rest of the restaurant disappeared from her view.

Masha put her faith in me—and I have failed.

Kat's mission priorities were out the window except for the final one—self-preservation.

Igor hadn't given her a weapon—not even a knife or some sort of hairpin. "Just in case they search you," he had explained.

She would have to make do with what she had.

With a foot to the stair railing, she pushed with all her strength, letting the man take her entire weight. An instant later, they were airborne.

The man cushioned her fall. She rolled off him, frantically searching for where his gun had gone when it skittered across the concrete floor.

No time.

Kat didn't stop to think. She and the other girls had spent hours practicing the deadly move. As the man lay on his back at the bottom of the stairs, struggling to get air back into his lungs, she took his head in her hands, twisted, and broke his neck.

The other two men had vanished.

There!

A small door was open in the corner of the basement.

A tunnel.

She wanted to kick off the ridiculous shoes to move silently but worried about leaving behind evidence of her involvement. She moved slowly instead, carefully placing each foot onto the dirty concrete floor of the basement, moving to the doorway.

With a quick pull, the ribbon came out of her hair. She wrapped it around both hands, stretching it tight between them before ducking into the dark opening of the tunnel.

The tunnel was black. Either there were no lights or the men hadn't turned them on in hopes of the darkness hiding them.

Kat snuck up behind the second man, hurrying ahead of her and bumping his head on the low ceiling of the tunnel every few steps.

She guessed his position and kicked with all her strength, her foot missing the mark but coming close enough to elicit a gasp of pain as the man dropped to his knees. She found the man's head in the darkness and slipped the ribbon around his neck.

It broke the second she tried to strangle him.

Kat tumbled backward—which saved her life.

The man recovered enough to fire his pistol. Bullets whizzed by and would have slammed into her body had she been standing or crouched.

When the shooting stopped, Kat sprang up and attacked.

It takes a surprising amount of effort to kill a man with your bare hands, she discovered. But the school—and the bullies when she was younger—had prepared her well.

She took her share of painful blows, but in the end, the man lay dead—the life choked out of him by her arm locked around his neck.

I should have just done that from the start.

The third man—the one with the briefcase and the files—was somewhere ahead of her in the tunnel.

5

THE DRESS

Many Years Earlier
Moscow, Russia

The last man was more alert—or better trained.

He shot her as she crept down the tunnel.

The bullet entered her left side with a flash of fire.

She ignored the pain, more angry about it than hurt.

Kat lunged to the side of the tunnel and rushed him.

He got off two more shots before she knocked the gun out of his hands.

It didn't take long after that.

More alert. Not better trained.

Kat left him lying in the dark. She felt around for the briefcase, found it, and confirmed it was still closed—and locked.

It took several painstaking minutes to search the man and to sweep the floor with her hands in the dark. She had to make sure the files and papers hadn't been taken from the case and tossed down the tunnel by the man or hidden in his clothing.

All the while, she bled.

Thankfully, the gun was easier to find. With it in one hand and the briefcase in the other, she stumbled back down the tunnel to the restaurant.

At some point, she had started crying. The tears mixed with mucus from her nose—but she did her best to ignore the pain.

Once back in the dim light of the basement, she assessed the damage. Her once-pristine white outfit was covered in dirt and blood.

The dress is ruined.

She wanted to laugh at the absurdity of her concern.

I'm in shock.

They'd had first aid training, but there wasn't much she could do for the gunshot.

Get to the rendezvous with the briefcase. That's all that matters.

She would do her duty and complete her mission—or die trying.

From the top of the stairs, Kat shot the bodyguard in the back of the head. He hadn't budged from his position at the door... and she didn't have the strength or time to deal with him any other way.

She stripped his suit coat off, pleased her shot had kept it mostly free of blood and gore.

It hung on her like a tent more than a big coat. The bottom edge brushed the ground, and she had to roll and roll the sleeves so her hands could stick out and grasp the briefcase. Still, it hid the dirty, bloody dress.

Better to look ridiculous, like she was wearing her father's coat, than to show anyone on the street that she'd been shot.

Kat held on until she reached the park, four blocks away.

Igor scooped her into his arms and rushed her into a panel van.

She wouldn't let go of the briefcase, even for him, until the darkness took her. She faded just as the van pulled away from the curb with Igor still cradling her.

6

THE COINCIDENCE

Sortavala, Russia

Ekaterina's tea had gone cold in her hands, but the fire was crackling and warm.

They sent me in without a weapon.

She accomplished the mission anyway.

Immediately, she became the star student and was given better food, extra training, and even a little deference from the staff.

Which led, year by year, assignment after assignment, death after death, to the tiny cabin in western Russia, an hour from the border with Finland.

Ekaterina wondered still if the school paid attention to such things —whether it was a fluke or by design that her first mission was on the anniversary of her parent's death… and the distraction was a car accident.

It could have been a coincidence…

It didn't matter.

She could never forgive them for making her what she had become.

The same way Moscow would never forgive her for walking away from the job and disappearing—if they ever figured out she was alive.

How long before they find me here in this cabin and pay me a visit?

She poked the logs in the fire, added another, and got up to make more tea.

7

THE KNOWING

Alex "Axe" Southmark's Cabin
Rural Virginia

Axe cleared his throat. He thought he had an answer to Mariana's question about when to kill—and when to hold back.

"Have you ever been in love?" he asked her.

"Yes, of course."

Across the room, Haley nodded slowly.

She gets it.

"Did you tell them?"

"Yes."

"You just knew, right?" Johnboy spoke up, surprising them all. The normally quiet man smiled shyly. "That feeling of being in love. When you know, you know."

"Every time I've killed someone," Axe said, "I knew it was the right thing to do. Obviously, killing is the very different from being in love, but that 'knowing' is the same."

"And if you don't feel that?" Mariana asked, her voice quiet.

"You don't pull the trigger," Axe said.

Once again, his thoughts turned to the older Russian woman he'd confronted in Los Angeles.

Would it have been better to kill her?

No.

It hadn't felt right.

Mad Dog raised his beer. For a second, Axe worried he'd make a joke or say something inappropriate, but Mad Dog said, "To always doing the right thing."

They all leaned forward to clink their bottles.

Axe checked in with Mariana, who looked satisfied that her question had been answered adequately.

"So no shit, there I was," Mad Dog started, leaning forward with a sly look on his face.

Axe listened to the man's story, but his thoughts stayed on the topic Tex had brought up.

Someday, if the shoe is on the other foot, my life might be spared by someone who also knows the difference between right and wrong—someone who knows when to pull the trigger... and when not to.

OPERATION BATTLE RATTLE

1

THE FEAR

Alex "Axe" Southmark's Cabin
Rural Virginia

The intel team—Nancy, Dave, and Marcus—had left in the wee hours of the morning, driven by a still-sober Gregory.

Like the other warriors: Johnboy, Mariana, and Haley—Mad Dog had elected to stay overnight at the cabin. It was too late—and they were all too tipsy to drive.

He commandeered the couch while Axe gathered sleeping bags, blankets, and pillows from the hall closet.

"Shouldn't you sleep in a chair?" Johnboy asked him with a smile. "You barely fill up the couch."

"Seniority," Mad Dog muttered as he stretched out. He'd been on Axe's team since the craziness on St. John, US Virgin Islands, when he swam for hours with all his gear to save Axe's ass.

Mad Dog didn't expect a challenge from JB. SEALs weren't known for their adherence to protocol, but they had their own internal hierarchy. A man's character, reputation, and experience counted for much more than rank.

Besides, either of them could have fallen asleep on a chair or the floor just as easily as a comfy old couch. They'd mastered the skill of choosing to fall asleep, shutting down, and resting whenever—and wherever—they could. Haley or Mariana could have the bed in the spare bedroom. He'd take a worn-out couch any day.

Mad Dog glanced around the room. Axe was in the hallway gathering the last of the blankets. JB settled back into a recliner, eyes half-closed in the dim light from the fireplace. Mariana and Haley weren't used to staying up all night and seemed half asleep.

Perfect time for this one.

"Let me tell you," Mad Dog said, "about one of the few times I've ever been truly afraid."

Axe came around the corner, dumped the blankets onto a spare chair, and took a seat in another. The ladies blinked their eyes and woke up quickly.

"Don't worry, this is a short one," Mad Dog said. "You know how it is: in the moment, when the bullets are flying, training takes over. Once in a while, though, especially before the action starts, fear can creep in. It's important to know how to deal with it."

He didn't think Mariana had felt an ounce of fear during their latest mission. None that had affected her actions, at least. Still, it would be good for her to hear the story if she wanted to stick with the team.

Mad Dog had everyone's attention now. The tale would go perfectly with some others that had been shared over the past months in this room. It was worth telling, even if it caused him nightmares later on. His body shivered just thinking about that night. He wondered if the others noticed, but he didn't look—he didn't want to know.

"So no shit, there I was," Mad Dog said, remembering. "I can't tell you where, of course, but it was an unusual op. We inserted a long way from the X, just before sunset. We had a brutal hike ahead of us..."

2

THE CANYON

Many Years Earlier
Somewhere in South America

Mad Dog had point. Three of his buddies followed, spaced well apart to avoid an ambush or harm from booby traps.

They were in a narrow slot canyon the intel team had identified as the best approach to the target.

"It's supposed to be impassable," the guy doing the intelligence briefing had explained, "but we have a source who claims that at this time of year, given the lack of recent rain, you can get through."

It would take extra time to climb over rocks and navigate the deep sand of a dry riverbed, but it beat the alternative. The enemy had mines, booby traps, and sentries in the rocks above the canyon. That way was riskier, the higher-ups had decided.

Of course, none of them were along on the mission, walking through the spooky canyon.

Easy for them to say this is the best approach, Mad Dog thought.

High above, the sun was setting, but in the canyon it was already dark.

Mad Dog stopped suddenly, his senses on high alert. He'd seen something in the green glow of the night vision goggles...

There. The barest hint of a tripwire—the third so far, and they'd barely gone half a mile.

He stood still, examining every inch of the path in front of him—the walls to the side, high, and low—looking for secondary booby traps.

Nothing. Or at least nothing that I can see.

If he missed one, at least the end would be quick.

Probably something as simple as a grenade, pin pulled, shoved in a crack in the rock to be yanked out when some idiot—like me—blunders through here.

He carefully stepped over the wire and found a stick to create a subtle reminder mark in case they had to return this way. If he was dead or otherwise not on point, it would signal to whoever led the way the need for care.

Before turning to continue the hike, Mad Dog pointed the wire out to the next SEAL coming up behind him, knowing he would do the same to the man following him.

After that, the way was easy. The enemy must have figured one of the three traps would catch anyone stupid enough to risk the canyon approach.

I'd put a sentry at the far end, though, just in case.

Sentries he could watch for, approach stealthily, and kill before they realized he was near them. Men on guard duty got tired and bored of looking at the same thing hour after hour, especially if nothing ever happened. Modern militaries had methods for dealing with this: rotating personnel on a regular basis, keeping guard times short and manageable, instilling high levels of commitment and drive for even the most boring assignments.

The men working for tonight's target were a diverse group of true believers, hired hands, and low-level goons.

It's not the top tier who gets the scut work of guarding a slot canyon all night.

Mad Dog bet the guard—if there was one—would be asleep by the time the SEALs arrived on target.

He won't be a problem.

It was ten minutes later when it became apparent why the canyon was actually considered impassible.

The canyon walls were about ten feet apart. The soft sand and gravel of the dry riverbed made for slow going. Each foot had to be placed carefully to ensure silence, just in case someone had gone to great effort and placed sentries farther from the target's base.

Mad Dog stalked down the middle of the canyon, five feet from either wall.

He placed his right foot down quietly and prepared to shift his weight—and froze.

The instant he heard the sound, he knew.

That's a rattlesnake—very close!

Turning only his head, he located the source of the sound. What he had first thought was a pile of branches was alive.

The rattle came again from the snake coiled near the base of the canyon wall.

Easy, fella...

Or was it a female?

Easy, lady... dude... whatever.

Knowing the snake didn't want to attack didn't help. The caveman part of his brain had taken over and held Mad Dog frozen.

Move.

The mission came first. One little snake wasn't going to stop them from taking out the target.

The snake rattled again. Somehow, it sounded angrier.

Mad Dog couldn't move.

They can strike three times their length... or is that just a myth?

If he held still for long enough, would the snake retreat?

We don't have that kind of time.

Slowly, Mad Dog forced his body to the left, taking the next step with the sheer will and determination that got him into the SEAL program and through BUD/S training, overcoming his base instincts that wanted him to ease his way backward and never set foot in another slot canyon again.

The rattle sounded again as soon as he moved—and didn't let up until Mad Dog had taken two more steps forward and closer to the far wall, giving the snake his—or her—space.

Mad Dog held his position and signaled to the SEAL behind him— call sign Jackpot—pointing to the spot where the snake rested.

That was a close one.

Ten more steps along the left wall brought him to the next snake and another loud, angry rattle.

3

THE HIKE

Alex "Axe" Southmark's Cabin
Rural Virginia

"Remember BUD/S?" Mad Dog asked Axe and Johnboy. "They threw everything at us! Gunfire. Flashbangs. Smoke. Yelling, screams, cries. After all that, combat was almost a letdown." He shook his head. "I swear, if they ever ask me to teach in Coronado, I'm bringing in rattlesnakes! Put them in plexiglass boxes with air holes and scatter them around the obstacle course at night. Let the next generation get a sense of the pucker fest I experienced."

"The snakes were more afraid of you than you were of them," Axe said.

"Bullshit! I was petrified. It took all I had to keep moving."

"How many were there?" Mariana asked.

"Or..." Haley spoke up. "You didn't turn around, did you?"

Mad Dog snorted. "Give up? No way. We had a job to do—a target had to die."

"When it absolutely, positively has to be dead overnight," Johnboy said.

"Exactly. So we kept right on going," Mad Dog said.

Many Years Earlier
Somewhere in South America

Mad Dog counted the snakes as he zigzagged his way up the canyon.

Twenty-three.

He eased to his right, giving the latest one as much room as he could. The canyon had narrowed and was now only six feet wide.

Another rattle from ahead.

Twenty-four.

Sweat trickled down his back.

He had the walk down to a science. The snakes didn't like being startled, so Mad Dog gave up on stealth. Instead, he scuffed his feet lightly, just enough to give a warning to the next snake. They would rattle once, then slither away by the time he moved forward.

All we need to do is give them a warning and time to move.

That worked well—but the approach to the target was taking much longer than they had allotted.

And the canyon walls kept closing in.

4

THE PRAYER

"I was actually more afraid of not completing the mission," Mad Dog said.

Axe and Johnboy both snorted.

"Yeah, right," JB said.

Mad Dog shrugged, conceding the lie. "Okay, not at first. But as the time slipped away, that became my concern. I had to weigh the odds of being bitten versus arriving too late to catch our target and take him out."

"People don't actually die from rattlesnake bites though, do they?" Mariana asked.

She's from Texas. She should know.

"It depends on the person, how much venom is released by the snake, and the time before treatment. If you get a high dose and don't get anti-venom in time, yeah, you can die. And we were a long way from home—and farther from a hospital that stocked anti-venom."

"So what did you do?" Axe asked.

"We did the same thing you would do," Mad Dog said.

Many Years Earlier
Somewhere in South America

Mad Dog prayed. He'd gone to church every Sunday as a kid, wearing those damn uncomfortable cheap nylon black socks his mom bought for him and the hand-me-down dress shoes that never fit right. Sunday school, the whole deal.

As an adult, he didn't know what he believed in—heaven, Valhalla, a Great Spirt, or a white tunnel to the beautiful afterlife—and he didn't worry much about it. He lived his life by a code, did the right thing because it was the right thing, not because of any particular belief system, and figured it would all work itself out once he was gone.

The snakes, though, had him reaching for any scripture that came to mind.

None of it felt right.

Finally, he stopped, waiting for the latest snake—number thirty-one —to slither away somewhere under the rock wall.

Mad Dog closed his eyes and prayed from the heart to whatever might be out there.

Please help me complete my mission without me or any of my guys getting bitten by snakes.

He felt a sense of peace. After a moment, he started forward again the same as before, making noise to give the snakes a heads-up he was coming, but moving faster.

They'll get out of the way, or they won't. We'll make it either way.

5

THE WAKE-UP

Alex "Axe" Southmark's Cabin
Rural Virginia

"It worked?" Mariana asked.

Mad Dog nodded. "We made good time after that. There were plenty of rattles from more snakes—thirty-three, to answer your question," he told Mariana. "But I moved at the pace I would have normally, given the possibility of sentries and more tripwires." He shook his head with a grin. "I passed within about two feet of one but just looked at it and shook my head. It stopped rattling. As I walked by, it slithered under the canyon wall."

"Were the other guys as freaked out as you?" Johnboy asked.

Mad Dog laughed. "Nope! Jackpot saw the first one I pointed out, but none of the others. The other guys didn't see any. They all wondered what the hell was taking me so long on point!"

"But the important question…" Axe said.

Axe: always the professional.

Mad Dog got serious. "Yes, we accomplished the mission. Scratch one more bad guy off the list."

Axe nodded at him. He nodded back.

"And on the way back? After the mission?" Mariana asked.

"They were gone. Off hunting or whatever." He shrugged and grinned. "All's well that ends well, I guess."

"Now, ladies and gentlemen," Mad Dog said with a stretch, "with that bedtime story, it's time for a nap. Sleep well, all."

He grabbed a sleeping bag off the pile on the nearby chair, draped it over himself, and settled back with his eyes closed. It would be dawn soon. They would sleep until late morning or early afternoon, have breakfast, and go for a run together before heading home.

Mad Dog set a mental alarm. He wanted to be up early, before the others. He'd noticed Axe's fancy coffee beans in the kitchen. Shaken gently inside the grinder, in the hallway, he bet they'd sound near enough like a rattlesnake to give Mariana—and hell, even Blondie or JB—a proper morning wake-up.

OPERATION SUDDEN FURY

1

REGRETS

Sortavala, Russia

Ekaterina stared into the fire, the novel on her lap long forgotten. The wind howled, but the one-room cabin was warm and cozy.

She had only a reading lamp on the small end table next to her wooden straight-back chair, but it provided plenty of light to push back the darkness and keep her company.

As the logs burned and flames danced, her thoughts turned once again this cold evening to her many regrets.

So many years in this business, and what do I have to show for them?

Instead of being surrounded by others of her kind—operators or, more specifically in her case, assassins—she hid in a tiny cabin an hour from the border of Finland.

I should never have left Los Angeles after failing my mission.

It was far from the first time she'd faced that particular regret. What had seemed like the perfect solution to escaping a life she'd long grown tired of now felt like a prison sentence. Not every day—most days were wonderful: drinking tea, reading by the fire, going for walks in the frigid cold, and, most importantly, not killing anyone.

She also no longer worried about dying.

Or worse: failing.

Failing—like I did in Los Angeles.

She had been given inadequate intel, selected a team, and made a plan based on the wrong information.

Still, it irked her.

Others hadn't done their jobs properly, which caused her to lose men, barely escape with her life, flee to this small town, buy the cabin, and retire, all without reporting to Moscow.

Most days were fine; she was happy with her retirement. But on nights like this, when her thoughts turned to past missions, she dreamt of being part of a team again.

Or even better—being on her own to accomplish the assignment with as much autonomy as possible. But either way, she dreamed of being back in the life she both hated and missed.

Ekat's thoughts turned from the failed final mission of her long career to what was technically her second operation, though she had always considered it the first genuine test of her abilities. She had been on her own and made all the life-and-death decisions.

On impulse, she found an old notebook and pen in a kitchen drawer left behind by the previous tenants of the cabin. In her business, it paid to never write down information. But tonight, just this once, she would get the story out. It wouldn't replace having a confidant, a peer to tell the tale, but she felt like doing more than reminiscing in her mind.

She took the pen, licked the tip to encourage the ink to flow, and remembered.

So there I was. Fourteen, and already a killer.

2

_____

FREEDOM

Sortavala, Russia

Only a few months had passed since the first mission—where I had my first kill. Four kills, actually. The school had sent me in, unarmed, wearing a pretty little girl's dress. No one was supposed to suspect me, but it all went wrong.

Ekat paused, anger suddenly burning as bright as the fireplace. She took a sip of tea, then resumed writing.

It was the anniversary of the death of my parents. I will never forgive the school for that, whether or not it was a coincidence.

But enough of that one. My second mission—that was for me. And, I suppose, for my country.

Masha had a sour face and disposition. She frowned, always. Except at the end.

She was the assistant director of the spy school and the person in charge of my first mission. No one liked her, but she did her job well and ran the school effectively, from what I saw as a child. The director was rarely around; Masha handled the day-to-day business of managing the teachers and handling the students.

After the success of that initial mission, I became the star of the school. People treated me differently, from the teachers to the students. Life became easier in many ways, except for how I felt.

At fourteen, I had followed my training and killed four men in one afternoon. I didn't understand then, but I was ill prepared to handle that day. I had yet to work through the mental damage caused by the sudden loss of my parents, let alone the impact of killing others.

One night, after waking from the nightmares, I dressed and, acting on instinct, slipped out of the school. This was not easy. There were guards and what was back then a high-tech security system. But they had trained me well. I treated it as additional training and would use that as my excuse if caught.

I had to get away. Be more than a killer, more than an asset in training.

I wore dark pants, a dark shirt, and a jacket against the chill. Once away from the building, I explored the surrounding neighborhood, returning safely, undetected, before dawn for a nap.

The next day at school passed with more peace and focus than I had felt in months.

Each night from then on, I would sleep a few hours, wake from the nightmares, use the restroom, then dress and slip out. I walked the dark streets of Moscow.

Free.

A week after my first escape, I was nearly caught by Masha as she left the school much later than usual. I blended into the shadows, as taught, and disappeared until she had passed on the other side of the street.

Something about the way she walked compelled me to follow. Or perhaps, knowing what I do now, it was intuition—the feeling of danger I have long since grown to recognize and trust.

To her credit, Masha employed a sophisticated surveillance detection routine as she walked. It took all my skill to follow her without giving myself away. She looped back, turning around in the middle of the block to return the way she'd come. On the subway, there were few people, forcing me to stay far away and risk losing her.

I had learned my lessons well, though. As good as she was, I knew I was better—and proved it that night.

After nearly an hour, Masha passed through a small neighborhood park. The residential area surrounding it looked nice to my young eyes. Not luxurious, but not an area of poverty. I suspected she lived nearby. Soon, I would know where she resided. The information might come in handy one day.

I stayed in the shadows at the edge of the park, watching Masha cut through the open area, appreciating her tradecraft. A team would be able to follow, but not easily. The streets around the park were deserted; a moving vehicle this late wouldn't be cause for alarm but would stick out.

A single person following her, as I did, would have to stay outside the park to avoid exposure. They—I—could risk going along the outside border and possibly miss her if she exited a different direction or retraced her steps.

I resigned myself to possibly losing her. There would be other opportunities to investigate the area and find her again, I knew.

Standing in darkness against the trunk of a wide tree, I waited and watched in the dim glow of the few working streetlights inside the park.

Between two lights, at the darkest point, Masha suddenly stumbled and fell to one knee. A second later, she stood, dusted herself off, and continued.

A trip. Common enough on the poorly maintained sidewalk, especially in the darkness.

My senses tingled. There was more to it than met the eye. People like Masha—and me—didn't slip. Didn't fall.

We were not clumsy.

3

SUSPICIONS

Sortavala, Russia

For a moment, I wondered if Masha had detected me long before and had used the trip to check on my location.

My intuition told me otherwise.

I stayed frozen against the tree, giving up on following Masha to her home. It had to be one of the apartment buildings nearby. I could find her later—she'd be at the school every day from morning to night. There would be many more chances to follow her or return to this park and wait for her to appear.

Remember, I was fourteen. I had been at the school for four years. And of course, I had killed. I wasn't a little girl, but I wasn't the operator I am now. In many ways, I was sheltered. I didn't have much life experience.

What I had, though, was advanced training in espionage and counterespionage.

I waited. I didn't fidget or move. I held my bladder. I felt like I had become one with the tree.

Two hours later, I got my reward.

A young man, in his twenties from the way he moved, walked casually across the park. He appeared to be a happy lover going home after a few hours with his girlfriend.

Even from that distance, I noted his untied shoe as he passed through the dim cone of light from one of the working streetlights.

He must have finally noticed it too—right as he reached the darkness between the two lights, where he stopped along the path. He kneeled and tied his shoe.

I was suspicious, of course. He had walked nearly halfway across the park and who knows how far from his lover's apartment before noticing his shoelace? He had to tie it in the exact spot Masha had tripped?

My vantage point prevented me from seeing the ground along the path, but I guessed there was a tree stump, rock, or some hiding place for a small item.

Yes, I worried I was wrong. Paranoid. But I knew what I had to do.

I had to kill the man, find out what Masha had left in a dead drop for him, and confirm my suspicion.

4

SKILLS

Sortavala, Russia

The suspicious stranger made it easy. He came directly toward me, keeping up the unhurried happy-late-night-stroll act.

My age and gender undoubtedly helped with the next part.

So, too, did the tears. Real. No acting required.

I slipped around the tree, unseen, using it to block his view of me.

I sat on the sidewalk, hugging my knees to my chest, face down, and thought of my parents. My old life, before they had died. How much different my world would have been had they lived.

The tears flowed.

The man had to stop, or at least pause. To do otherwise would have been suspicious.

"Are you all right?" he asked in flawless Russian. Most Muscovites wouldn't notice the slight accent or would have passed it off as him being from Ukraine. I'm sure he had a story, an excuse if anyone asked.

I didn't ask. The accent confirmed my suspicions. I had spent four years studying English, French, German, and Spanish, including how to minimize my Russian accent. I pegged him as an American.

A spy.

I jumped as if startled and looked up at him, twenty feet away, where he'd stopped—reluctantly, I thought.

"Sorry, didn't mean to scare you," he said. He was handsome in a way. Thin. Wiry, like a runner.

"My dog," I mumbled. He stepped a few feet closer and leaned in to hear me. "I lost my dog. Have you seen her? A puppy," I said.

"A puppy?" he asked. "No, I haven't seen one." He looked relieved and stepped away.

"Will you help me look for her?" I asked as I stood and walked to him, making my face look desperate and pleading. "I took her out and she ran away."

I only had to keep the ruse alive long enough to close the distance, and it was working.

"My parents are going to be so angry," I said as I reached him.

He didn't want to help. He was suspicious. A young girl, all alone at this time of night, crying at the edge of the park where his dead drop was located?

But I looked so harmless. Short, thin to the point of scrawniness, yet pretty, so the instructors at the school claimed.

He hesitated—and I struck.

The kick caught him where a man least wants to be kicked. He choked out a gasp as he bent forward.

I smashed his face with my knee.

He dropped to the ground.

Leaning forward, I took his neck in my hands and twisted until it snapped.

It took only a few seconds. And, God help me—if there is a God, and if He is still willing to help me after all I've done—I felt proud of my skills.

The film canister—remember those?—was in his right jacket pocket. I took it, his wallet, keys, and watch.

This took a few seconds more.

I left him as he lay on the sidewalk next to the park and made my way back to the school.

5

PAPER

I hid the man's possessions in the girls' bathroom. Had they been found, I would have been the natural primary suspect, but there were other girls who had my skills. Any of them could have snuck out and robbed someone.

No one looked.

I spent the day worried I had acted rashly and killed an innocent man.

After dinner the next evening, I retreated to the bathroom and retrieved the film canister.

Inside were thin pieces of paper—air mail stationery—with descriptions of every girl in the school... in Masha's careful handwriting. Hair color, eye color, body type, moles or scars, special skills, primary focus—spy, seductress, assassin—and more. Every little detail about us, meant especially to identify who we were, and including the next week's schedule for public training, where we emerged from the school to practice tradecraft of all sorts on the streets of Moscow.

With this information, the man I had killed would have been able to track us, know who we were, take photographs, and gain insight into the next generation of female operators to emerge from the school.

I had been right.

The kill had been justified.

Which left Masha.

6

DEATH

Sortavala, Russia

I followed Masha that night, just in case she had more information to deliver to whomever—the Americans, I guessed.

I waited thirty minutes after she entered her apartment before picking the door with tools stolen from the school.

She lay on her back in the small, one-room apartment, already snoring.

When I opened the kitchen drawer, she stirred but didn't awaken.

With my hand over her mouth, I pushed the paring knife into her throat. Not far. Only several centimeters. Not enough to kill her.

She woke, her wide eyes immediately alert. They found mine as I leaned over her.

"Don't scream," I told her. "I don't want to have to kill your neighbors, too."

Masha held perfectly still. The knife tip had to hurt, but she didn't cry out. I kept my hand in place anyway.

"I killed the American," I said. A twitch on her face confirmed I had guessed correctly. "Is anyone else at the school in on it?"

She shook her head the tiniest amount.

I hesitated then. Remember, I was fourteen. "I... I think I have to kill you," I said, and paused. "Right?" It felt strange to ask her permission, but wrong not to.

As I've heard the Americans say in the years since, the decision was "way above my pay grade."

Masha's eyes were sad, but she nodded once.

Right before the pain came, she had another expression.

Pride. She was proud of me.

Once she was gone, I quietly ransacked the apartment, stole some cheap jewelry and a small amount of money, and left, leaving the front door a few centimeters open.

I discarded the knife and jewelry on the way back to the school.

The next day, Masha didn't show up for work.

While there were many rumors and stories made up by the other girls, no one ever gave an official answer as to where Masha had gone. In time, they promoted one of the instructors to assistant director.

And I continued my path to becoming... what I became.

Ekaterina put down the pen and stretched her tired hand, wiggling the fingers, clenching and unclenching her fist.

It felt good to get the story out.

Setting the notebook on the end table, she stood and added one more log to the hot coals. After a moment, it caught fire.

She sat down with a sigh and sipped her tea, which had grown cold, before picking up the notebook again.

Saving the papers wasn't an option. No one could read the story.

There was only one thing to do.

Ekat carefully ripped the pages from the notebook and fed them, one by one, to the fire.

OPERATION CEASE FIRE

1

THE GAME

The White House
The Executive Residence

President James Heringten leaned back in the easy chair and took another sip of beer. The presidential residence on the second floor of the White House was quiet and still, though outside the door on the far side of the room, two Secret Service agents stood—as always.

Other agents patrolled the building and the grounds.

In the kitchen, staff would be on standby in case the president or his guest needed a midnight snack.

The First Lady had already gone to bed after sharing a small glass of wine and catching up with James's Chief of Staff and longtime friend, Chad David. James didn't often invite his longtime friend up to have a drink, but tonight there were things he needed to get off his chest.

The television was on, the volume low. Next to him, in the matching easy chair, Chad sipped his beer. Together, they watched the end of a game neither was very interested in. The evening was an excuse to chat informally, away from the Oval Office, the Situation

Room, and the immediate pressures of whatever crisis of the day they had to deal with.

"You going to tell me what's bothering you now, or are we waiting until the end of the game?" Chad asked, eyes stuck on the TV.

He knows me well, James thought.

"China? North Korea?" Chad asked.

"Haley," James said.

"Ah." The younger man, who had been at James's side through combat as a SEAL and through the political fights of Washington for five years—including the two presidential campaigns—as well as his time as a senator before, said nothing else.

He's waiting to see which way the wind is blowing.

Chad had great political instincts. He'd wait to see James's attitude before telling him exactly what he thought, whether he wanted to hear it or not. Knowing James's take on the subject, though, would shape how he presented his opinions.

James chuckled quietly.

Chad glanced at him. "What?"

"I was just remembering that first big negotiation," James said. "You remember?"

Chad nodded. "How could I forget?"

They lapsed into silence, lost in thought. James took another sip of beer and remembered the steady chatter of the machine gun and the rounds zipping by. The return fire of his guys' weapons.

And the sudden, sure knowledge that if he and Chad didn't get off the street and behind cover immediately, they'd die—and the mission would go downhill from there.

2

CONTACT

Many Years Earlier
Somewhere In the Middle East

"Contact front!" came from the radio, barely heard over the sound of a heavy weapon—a machine gun mounted on a vehicle, from the sounds of it and the speed at which it moved down the street perpendicular to them.

No shit, James thought.

The small town in the dusty, impoverished country contained mostly civilians. A small but powerful group of men, along with their leader, kept the peace and had served as the de facto government since the nation's political parties had succumbed to bitter verbal warfare before descending into assassinations and full-scale civil war in and around the capital.

Out here, in the rural part of the country, strong criminals took the opportunity presented by the weakened central government to grab power.

Taxes, fees, and bribes that had once gone to the local government and police now came directly to them. They were the law, the police, and the army wrapped together.

And, unfortunately, James and his team's attempt to sneak quietly into a neighborhood, snatch their primary target, and get out without being discovered had gone horribly wrong from the start.

So now, no shit, there they were with a machine gun sending death in their direction.

James acted on instinct, throwing his body at the door to the nearest house, praying his mass would be enough to shatter the lock, the hinges, or the door itself.

3

CEASE FIRE

Many Years Earlier
Somewhere In the Middle East

James stumbled into a large room as the door gave way. He dived to
the ground, desperate to get out of the line of fire from the machine
gun up the street.

Behind him, Chad—call sign "Dino"—flew in after him.

He was ready for a family huddled in a corner, riding out the
sudden gunfire, or a few tangos readying an attack from the Team's
rear.

What confronted James made his blood go cold.

At least a dozen armed men lay on the floor, staying low to avoid
the occasional machine gun round through the thin mud walls of the
home.

As James and Chad landed in the room, the tangos trained their
weapons on the two SEALs.

Over the noise of the gunfire outside, an angry voice yelled in a
room off to the side. James hadn't picked up much of the language, but
he caught what he thought was a variation of the word, "stop."

I think that's something like, "Cease fire!"

The machine gun stopped, though James's SEALs didn't.

All this happened in an instant.

"Hold!" James yelled, hoping Chad had the same sense he did. If either of them opened fire, they'd take out a few of the tangos.

But they'd get shredded in the process.

"Copy," Chad said from next to him on the floor, sounding calm and in control.

Good man.

The tangos glared at James—but no one fired.

One man yelled through a doorway into the next room, a rapid, frantic sentence.

He's saying, "Boss, the bad guys came for dinner!"

4

THE NEGOTIATION

The White House
The Executive Residence

James chuckled.

"What?" Chad asked.

"Remember the look on that guy's face when he walked into the room and saw us lying on the floor in the middle of his warriors?"

Chad nodded. "Can you imagine what he thought?"

"I lived it and still can't believe we lived through it."

James stared at the TV, not seeing the game, as he remembered the night his life changed.

Many Years Earlier
Somewhere In the Middle East

The gunfire outside died down—James's SEALs no longer had targets.

A burly man with a thick black beard poked his head around the corner of the doorway, cautiously looking into the room.

His eyes widened as they met James's. He gasped, recovered, and started cursing under his breath.

He barked a question at the men in the room.

"Truce," one in the corner called out in heavily accented English.

"Truce," the burly man repeated, staring at James. It was half question, half offer.

What the hell is going on? Still, better a truce than a face full of bullets.

"Truce," James said firmly, with a nod. The intel team didn't have a picture of the local warlord—Kadyn Safar—but James knew the man was short, stocky, and had a thick beard—exactly like the person in front of him.

He was the Team's secondary target for this evening's raid.

What now?

The warlord once again barked out a fast string of orders to his men. They complied—reluctantly—and pointed their weapons away from James and Chad. Each man then slowly stood, making no sudden moves.

"Stand down," James said to Chad as he also got to his feet, keeping his M4 pointed at the ground and his finger off the trigger.

The warlord spoke into a small walkie-talkie. When he finished, he gestured in the direction the gunfire had come from. "Truce," he repeated.

James nodded and keyed his mic. "Charlie One Actual to all units. Cease fire. Say again: cease fire. Set up defensive positions and hold in place." He paused, hardly believing he was about to say this. "We have a temporary truce with the tangos. All units, how copy?"

One by one, the team leads of the large unit acknowledged.

James nodded at Kadyn. "Truce."

They were safe for now, and at least a few of the SEALs would be focused on the doorway behind James and Chad, ready to attack if needed.

No man left behind.

A thin, younger-looking man moved slowly across the back of the room to stand next to Kadyn.

That's the guy who speaks English.

With a few more orders, four chairs and a table were brought in from the next room.

Kadyn gestured for James and Chad to sit, which they did— moving slowly and carefully. No sudden movements.

Absolutely surreal.

Kadyn sat opposite James. The young man sat across from Chad. They stared at each other in silence for several seconds, until another of the warriors, his AK-47 slung over his shoulder, hurried in with a tall teapot and four mugs. He poured for James first, Chad second, Kadyn third, and the younger man last before returning to the other room.

The rest of Kadyn's men stood respectfully against the walls of the main room, surrounding the table.

James sipped his tea, expecting to hate it but liking the taste.

"Why? Here?" Kadyn said in accented English. "Me? Kill?"

James considered lying for a second before deciding against it. He was an excellent poker player, scoring big with at least one bluff per session. But bluffing worked best with knowledge of his opponent— and the other players assuming they had James all figured out.

"Yes—and no," James said.

Kadyn said something in his language which the kid translated, "Continue. Explain."

How much could he say without giving away operational intelligence?

Screw it. I'm sure they know by now who and what we're after.

"First, we want Haziqa Aydin," James said, naming the bomb maker who had been training others. His bombs targeted UN peacekeepers who were stationed in the capital city, trying to keep the peace and prevent civilian deaths.

"Haziqa," Kadyn said with disgust in his voice. The kid translated what else he said. "You can have him. He is bad. Evil."

Kadyn gestured, the universal sign for, "What else?"

"Second—you."

Kadyn nodded. "Why me?"

"You protect Haziqa. Your men steal from locals. Help others who harm civilians in the capital."

The kid translated. Kadyn shook his head angrily and spoke at length.

The kid's face scrunched up, and he mumbled an apology to Kadyn before turning to James. "We negotiate peace. USA and Kadyn." The kid mangled the pronunciation of "negotiate," but James figured it out.

Do I have the authority to negotiate anything?

James and Kadyn, through the somewhat limited English of the kid, spoke for hours, discussing the finer points of the local area, the nation, its civil war, and the politics involved.

By dawn, when James and Chad stepped out of the home, the warlord and the SEAL had agreed on a tentative deal. First, there would be peace and fair government for the village and region.

Next, James had an insider's insight on a potential solution to the country's overall situation. Kadyn was well connected and willing to help all parties work toward peace.

Plus, Kadyn was willing to relay the exact location where Haziqa— the bomb maker—would be the next night.

James and Chad led the SEAL Team as they exfilled, walking along the streets in broad daylight with no one shooting at them—both a rarity.

5

THE PROBLEM

The White House
The Executive Residence

James looked at Chad. "You remember what you told me that morning?"

That was the start of all this.

Chad nodded. "Of course. I asked if you'd ever consider running for office. With diplomatic skills like that, you'd be a natural." He shook his head with a smile. "You said you might make a good small-town mayor."

James shrugged. "I probably would have." He gestured at the room, taking it all in. "Thanks, by the way. I wouldn't be here if it weren't for you."

"You're welcome. Thanks for bringing me along for the ride." Chad paused, then asked, "So. Haley?"

What I invited him up here to discuss.

"Yes. I worry—for her, and about what's in her head."

"I know she's not a blood relation, but she's spent enough time around you for some of it to rub off. And given her time with Alex Southmark and the experiences they've shared, she's in good hands."

James took a slow, deep breath and released it slowly.

He's right.

James remembered Haley as a little girl, playing chess across from him after dinner when her parents visited, back when he was just beginning his political career. The thought of something happening to her out in the field made him sick to his stomach.

On the other hand, she was one of America's top analysts and a damn good field agent. How could he deny her the opportunity to live her life, no matter how it turned out?

As President of the United States, however, he felt duty-bound to keep Haley—and the knowledge she had of America's secrets—from falling into the hands of the enemy. The same way he wouldn't allow her boss, Gregory, to work as an operator, or any other analyst with knowledge.

Haley shouldn't be going into the field either.

"If it were me," Chad continued, "I'd give her space. She'll make the right call."

James waited. His Chief of Staff had more to say than that.

"And," Chad continued after several seconds, "I'd probably ask the CIA, Secret Service, or whoever to provide a few gizmos. A tracker, like the ones you wear when we're on the move."

James had several devices available to use when he traveled. They showed where he was at all times—from belt buckles to watches, lapel pins to a tiny transmitter that could be glued to his scalp.

If he was away from the White House, he wore multiple trackers.

"I'd also get her a pill," Chad said.

It took James a moment to catch on.

"We haven't made suicide pills in decades," James said, his voice quieter.

"We still have a supply of shellfish poison on hand. It wouldn't be difficult."

"You checked?"

"I figured this might come up at some point."

He's way ahead of me.

It didn't take James long to decide. "Do it. Quietly. Make it a research project. Get a variety of trackers. If she can't stick to the office, at least let's have a chance of finding her quickly if we need to."

He'd move heaven and earth to get her back safely if she ever fell into the hands of the enemy—or he'd launch a missile at where she was being held if he thought there was no hope of saving her.

Let's just pray it doesn't ever come to that.

"That's it?" Chad asked. "I thought there was something else on your mind."

James shook his head, marveling at the man's perception. "I've been thinking about my legacy."

"You've got time before your second term ends," Chad argued. "Plenty more to accomplish."

"True."

Does he get where I'm going with this?

"Oh," Chad said after a second. "You're wondering what to do about the Central Analysis Group—and the World Intelligence Agency, with Axe and Haley—once you're out of office."

"Nailed it."

For once, Chad didn't have a quick answer.

They sat in silence for a few minutes, pondering the problem.

Disband the team? Tell the next president about my semi-legal clandestine direct-action group? Or let them go ahead on their own, completely off the books, back to being unsanctioned assets?

"Hmm," Chad muttered. "Well, I guess we have three years to figure out a solution."

"Three years," James agreed.

But in the back of his mind, he couldn't help thinking about how close he'd come to losing his life recently during the State of the Union address, plus all the other dangers facing him personally—and the United States of America.

We never have as much time as we think.

AUTHOR'S NOTE

Thank you so much for reading these short stories. I hope you've enjoyed getting to know the characters better.

Please check out my other series by searching for my name on Amazon or typing this link into your browser window:

https://geni.us/T-R-1

Are you up to date on Axe and Haley's thrilling ops? Type this short link into your browser window:

https://geni.us/TeamSeries

I'm active on social media, sharing photos (like Axe would take!), writing progress updates, and random thoughts. I also ask for input on character names, plot points, or reader preferences as I'm writing the next book or story, so please follow me and help out.

Find me here:

Facebook: https://www.facebook.com/AuthorBradLee

Instagram: https://www.instagram.com/bradleeauthor/

Finally, license was taken in describing places, units, tactics, and military capabilities. Where technical issues and the story conflicted, I prioritized the story.

Made in the USA
Las Vegas, NV
06 May 2024

89614230R00173